PENGUIN BOOKS

Readings for Remembrance

Eleanor Munro edited the anthology *Wedding Readings*, which is available from Penguin. Among her books are *Originals: American Women Artists*, *Memoir of a Modernist's Daughter*, and *On Glory Roads: A Pilgrim's Book About Pilgrimage*. Her essays and criticism appear in the national and art press, and she lectures widely. Eleanor Munro lives in New York City.

Readings *for* Remembrance

A Collection for Funerals and Memorial Services

Selected and with an Introduction by
Eleanor Munro

Penguin Books

PENGUIN BOOKS
Published by the Penguin Group
Penguin Putnam Inc., 375 Hudson Street,
New York, New York 10014, U.S.A.
Penguin Books Ltd, 27 Wrights Lane,
London W8 5TZ, England
Penguin Books Australia Ltd, Ringwood,
Victoria, Australia
Penguin Books Canada Ltd, 10 Alcorn Avenue,
Toronto, Ontario, Canada M4V 3B2
Penguin Books (N.Z.) Ltd, 182–190 Wairau Road,
Auckland 10, New Zealand

Penguin Books Ltd, Registered Offices:
Harmondsworth, Middlesex, England

First published in Penguin Books 2000

1 3 5 7 9 10 8 6 4 2

LIBRARY OF CONGRESS CATALOGING-IN-PUBLICATION DATA
Readings for remembrance : a collection for funerals and memorial
services / selected and with an introduction by Eleanor Munro.
p.   cm.
Includes bibliographical references and index.
ISBN 0 14 02.8064 2
1. Death—Literary collections.   2. Funeral rites and ceremonies
Handbooks, manuals, etc.   3. Memorial rites and ceremonies Handbooks,
manuals, etc.   4. Memorial service Handbooks, manuals, etc.   5. Funeral
services Handbooks, manuals, etc.   6. Bereavement—Literary collections.
7. Grief—Literary collections.   I. Munro, Eleanor C.
PN6071.D4R42   2000
808.8'03548—dc21   99-39113

Printed in the United States of America
Set in Cochin
Designed by Patrice Sheridan

Acknowledgments

Viking Penguin editor Caroline J. White initiated this project and kindly kept me at it during a time when I was coming out of an incapacitating mourning period myself. Now behind each page of the book, in each poetic word and image, I remeet the blithe, fervent spirit of my son Lexy, who died in 1993, and also the presence of his brother David, who assembled his memorial service and contributed to it an unforgettable eulogy:

"By the rivers of Babylon—," David began,

"I sat down, and there I wept
when I remembered Zion . . .
For my captors asked me for mirth, saying
'Sing us one of the songs of Zion!'
[But] how could I sing the Lord's song
in a foreign land?"

David then drew out the trope of trying to sing in a foreign land, intimating that Lexy's illness had been a kind of exile from the land in which we all stood reaching for him. There was power in that image which has stayed with me to this day.

Along the way, friends and acquaintances suggested readings out of their own experiences for a volume like this. Also, more than a few loved friends have left our midst during these years, and I've taken inspiration from services arranged in their memories, and so the circle joins and enlarges.

Thanks, then, to many, including John Appleton, Patricia Blake, Francis Booth, Georges and Anne Borchardt, Ruth Bowman, Nancy Cardozo, Joan Lebold Cohen, Margaret Croyden, Joanna Fabris, Elizabeth Falk, Joan Fox, Mary Frank, Judy Feiffer, Carol Green, Joan Halperin, Philip Hamburger, Mary Stewart Hammond, Marjorie Iseman, Charles Jencks, Sally Jones, Sam and Francine Klagsbrun, Janet Klion, Margaret Kornfeld, Richard Kuhns, Stanley Kunitz, B. J. Lifton, David Lindstrom, Richard Miller, Ashley Davis Prend, Kevin Prufer, Jeannette Rohatyn, Phyllis Schimel, Eileen Simpson, Elisabeth Munro Smith, Patrick Smith, Naomi Halperin Spigle, Rev. James E. Thomas, Aileen Ward, Rev. John David Warren, Nancy Dingman Watson, Clyde Watson, and Christopher and Nancy Wood. Anna Vilenchitz provided editorial help, Mary Dalton-Hoffman assembled the permissions to reprint, and designer Patrice Sheridan, production editor Barbara Campo, and copy editor John Jusino created a book visually graceful in the hand.

Contents

Acknowledgments   vii
Introduction   1

Why We Gather   13

EURIPIDES   14
C. P. CAVAFY, "For Ammonis, Who Died at 29,
    in 610"   15
From a funeral service in *The Union Prayerbook*   15
MICHEL DE MONTAIGNE, from *The Autobiography*   16
JOHN MILTON, from "Lycidas"   17
SAMUEL JOHNSON, from *The Letters*   17
GERARD MANLEY HOPKINS, "Spring and Fall: To a
    Young Child"   18
EMILY DICKINSON
    "There's a certain slant of light"   19
    "The bustle in a house"   19
LEO TOLSTOY, from *What Men Live By*   20
GEORGE GORDON, LORD BYRON, "So, We'll Go No
    More A-Roving"   20
A. E. HOUSMAN, "We'll to the Woods No More"   21
JOHN HOLLANDER, "An Old-Fashioned Song"   21
DOROTHY WORDSWORTH, from the *Journal*   22
WALT WHITMAN, from "A Clear Midnight"   23
WALTER SAVAGE LANDOR, "Finis"   24

LI PO

   "Lady Wang-Chao—II"   25

   "On Seeing Off Meng Hao-Jan"   25

CONSTANCE EGEMO, "The Gathering"   26

E. M., from *Memoir of a Modernist's Daughter*   27

CHRISTOPHER NORTH (JOHN WILSON),

   from "A Fairy's Funeral"   27

PHILIP LEVINE, from "On the Meeting of

   García Lorca and Hart Crane"   28

HANNAH ARENDT   29

WILLIAM CARLOS WILLIAMS, "Tract"   29

MARK VAN DOREN, "What Now?"   32

Raw Grief and Bitter Mourning   33

HOMER, from *The Odyssey*   34

CATULLUS   35

HORACE   35

From the Yom Kippur morning service in

   The Union Prayerbook   35

SAINT AUGUSTINE, from *The Confessions*

   from "On the Death of His Mother"   36

   from "On the Death of a Friend"   37

WILLIAM DUNBAR, from "Lament for the Makers"   38

JOHN CLARE

   "An Invite, to Eternity"   40

   "I Am"   41

BEN JONSON

   from "Cynthia's Reve"   42

   "On my first son"   42

ANNE BRADSTREET, from "In Memory of My Dear
    Grandchild Elizabeth Bradstreet . . ."   43
ALFRED, LORD TENNYSON   43
MARY WOLLSTONECRAFT   43
WALTER DE LA MARE, "Even in the Grave"   43
RALPH WALDO EMERSON, from "Threnody"   44
PERCY BYSSHE SHELLEY, from "Adonais: An Elegy
    on the Death of John Keats"   45
ANONYMOUS   46
Japanese Poems
    EMPEROR HORIKAWA   48
    EMPEROR HANAZONO   48
    THE PRIEST FUJIWARA NO TOSHINARI   48
    YAKAMOCHI   49
    AKAHITO   49
    THE EMPRESS YAMATOHIME   49
GERARD MANLEY HOPKINS
    from "No worst, there is none"   50
    from "I wake and feel the fell of dark"   50
EMILY DICKINSON, "After great pain"   51
WINTU, "We Spirits Dance"   51
JAMES JOYCE
    from "The Dead"   52
    from *Finnegans Wake*   53
WILLIAM BLAKE, "On Another's Sorrow"   53
THOMAS HARDY
    from "The Walk"   56
    from "The Voice"   56
FRANCIS WILLIAM BOURDILLON, "Light"   57
W. H. AUDEN, "Funeral Blues"   57
WILFRED OWEN, "Anthem for Doomed Youth"   58

ROBERT LOWELL, "The Dead in Europe"   58

PAUL CELAN, from "Death Fugue"   59

STEVIE SMITH, "By a Holm-Oak"   60

Spiritual   61

JUDITH DUERK, from *Circle of Stones: A Woman's Journey to Herself*   61

EDNA ST. VINCENT MILLAY, "Time does not bring relief"   62

LOREN EISELEY, from *All the Strange Hours*   62

T. S. ELIOT, from "East Coker"   63

JAMES LAUGHLIN, "Are You Still Alone"   64

ADRIENNE RICH, "Tattered Kaddish"   64

DONALD HALL, "A Grace"   65

DYLAN THOMAS, "Do not go gentle into that good night"   65

THEODORE ROETHKE, "In a Dark Time"   66

ANNIE DILLARD, from *The Living*   67

FEDERICO GARCÍA LORCA, "And Then"   68

Mysteries: What Is Death? What Are Time, Space, Transformation?   69

CALDERÓN   70

PLATO, from *The Apology of Socrates*   71

CATO, from "Soliloquy on Immortality"   72

LUCRETIUS, from *On the Nature of the Universe*   72

OVID, from *Metamorphoses*   74

EPICTETUS, from *The Manual*   74

CHUANG TZU, from "The Mysterious Tao," in *Musings of a Chinese Mystic*   75

MARCUS AURELIUS, from *Meditations*   75

SHAKESPEARE, from *Julius Caesar*   76

BLAISE PASCAL, from the *Pensées*   77

JOHN STUART MILL   77

GASTON BACHELARD   77

LEIGH HUNT, from a letter on the death of
    John Keats   77

WALT WHITMAN   78

ALBERT EINSTEIN, from a letter on the death of
    physicist M. Besso   78

MARTIN BUBER, from "Here Where One Stands"   78

EDMOND JABES, from *The Book of Margins*   79

RAINER MARIA RILKE, from "Requiem"   80

American Indian Poems

    from the Papago   81

    from the Aztec   81

    from the Maya   81

W. SOMERSET MAUGHAM   82

HENRY JAMES

    from the *Notebook*   83

    from "The Altar of the Dead"   84

T. S. ELIOT, from "Little Gidding"   84

LADY WILDE, "The Black Lamb"   85

ROBERT FROST, "Nothing Gold Can Stay"   86

AUTHOR UNKNOWN, "Nothing that ever flew"   86

CZESLAW MILOSZ, from "On Parting with
    My Wife, Janina"   86

MARILYNNE ROBINSON, from *The Death of Adam*   87

EDMOND JABES, from *The Book of Margins*   87

THEODORE ROETHKE, from "The Lost Son"   87

Heroes and Heroines, Great and Simple 89

SAPPHO   90
From "The Death of Enkidu" in *Gilgamesh*   91
OVID, from "The Death of Phaethon"   93
SAPPHO, "Epitaph"   94
PLATO, from *The Phaedo*   95
C. P. CAVAFY, from "The Horses of Achilles"   97
THUCYDIDES
    from *History of the Peloponnesian War*   97
SOPHOCLES, from *Oedipus the King*   100
VIRGIL, from *The Aeneid*   100
From *Beowulf*   101
FRANÇOIS VILLON, "The Ballad of Dead Ladies"   101
ALFRED, LORD TENNYSON, from *Idylls of the King*   102
SHAKESPEARE
  from *Richard II*   105
  from *Julius Caesar*   105
  from *Julius Caesar*   105
  from *Hamlet*   106
BEN JONSON, on Shakespeare   106
LADY CATHERINE DYER, "My Dearest Dust"   107
ABRAHAM COWLEY, from "On the Death of
    Mr. William Hervey"   108
MIGUEL DE CERVANTES, from *Don Quixote*   108
CHRISTINA ROSSETTI, "Remember"   109
CHARLES WOLFE, from "The Burial of Sir John
    Moore at Coruña"   109
ROBERT LOUIS STEVENSON, "Requiem"   110
STANLEY KUNITZ
    from "A Blessing of Women"   110

RALPH WALDO EMERSON

    from "Self-Reliance"   112

    Inscription for a well in memory of the martyrs

        of the war   112

WALT WHITMAN, "A March in the Ranks

    Hard-Prest, and the Road Unknown"   112

LIEUTENANT COLONEL GEORGE FRANCIS ROBERT

    HENDERSON, "The Death of Stonewall

    Jackson"   114

W. B. YEATS, "Swift's Epitaph"   115

RUDYARD KIPLING, "The Widower"   115

WILLIAM CARLOS WILLIAMS,

    "The Widow's Lament in Springtime"   116

HENRY WADSWORTH LONGFELLOW

    from "A Psalm of Life"   117

WILLIAM JOHNSON-CORY, "Heraclitus"   118

MARCEL PROUST

    from *The Past Recaptured*   118

HENRY ADAMS, on Jefferson   121

WINSTON CHURCHILL

    from a letter to his wife   121

JOHN McCRAE, "In Flanders Fields"   122

RANDALL JARRELL, "A Field Hospital"   122

SAMUEL MENASHE, "The friends of my father" 124

ROBERT HAYDEN, "Those Winter Sundays"   124

E. E. CUMMINGS, "Buffalo Bill 's"   125

CLYDE WATSON, "Portrait (modelled after

    ee cummings)"   125

NANCY DINGMAN WATSON, "you came to me" 125

JEAN GARRIGUE, "For J."   127

PHILIP LARKIN, "In times when nothing stood" 127

Contents   [xv]

Timeless Praise in Scripture and Verse 129

PRAXÍLLA OF SÍCYON 130

From "Prayer for Osiris," rendered by Otto Eberhard 131

Genesis 11:1–9 (King James Version) 131

Isaiah 54:7–13 (King James Version) 132

From a funeral service in *The Union
 Prayerbook* 132

The Kaddish 133

Psalms (King James Version)

 from Psalm 8 135

 from Psalm 42 135

 from Psalm 90 136

 Psalm 121 137

Ecclesiastes 3:1–8 (King James Version) 137

Matthew 5:4 (King James Version) 138

DANTE ALIGHIERI, from *The Divine Comedy: The
 Paradiso* 138

BLACK ELK, from *Black Elk Speaks* 139

GERARD MANLEY HOPKINS, "Pied Beauty" 139

WILLIAM PENN, from "Union of Friends" 140

From "Amazing Grace" 140

JOHN GREENLEAF WHITTIER, from "The Eternal
 Goodness" 141

JOHN HENRY NEWMAN, from "The Pillar of the
 Cloud" 141

ISAAC WATTS, from "O God, Our Help" 142

Buddhist aphorism, from *The Dhammapada* 142

LAO-TZU, from the *Tao Te Ching* 143

CHUANG TZU, from *Musings of a Chinese Mystic* 143

Hindu teachings, from *The Upanishads* 144

SAINT FRANCIS OF ASSISI, from *The Mirror of Perfection* 146

GEORGE HERBERT
  "Virtue"   148
  from "Man"   148
HENRY VAUGHAN
  from "Friends Departed"   151
  from "The Night"   152
JOHN DONNE, "Death, be not proud"   152
PERCY BYSSHE SHELLEY, from "Adonais" 152
WILLIAM WORDSWORTH, from "Ode:
    Intimations of Immortality from
    Recollections of Early Childhood" 154
W. B. YEATS, from "Sailing to Byzantium" 155
EZRA POUND, from "Canto CXIV" 155
RUDYARD KIPLING, "L'envoi" 156
HENRY FRANCIS LYTE, "Eventide" 156
RAINER MARIA RILKE, "Buddha in Glory" 157

Meditations on Wisdom Coming Slowly   159

W. B. YEATS
  from "Vacillation"   160
JAMES JOYCE   161
Ninth-century lyric written for the
    Abbess of Grandestine   161
From *Everyman*   161
EDMUND SPENSER, from *The Faerie Queen* 162
WILLIAM FULLER, "Evening Hymn" 162
HENRY KING
  from "A Contemplation upon Flowers" 162
ALEXANDER POPE, from *An Essay on Man* 163
PERCY BYSSHE SHELLEY, "To _____" 164

EDWARD FITZGERALD

    from *The Rubáiyát of Omar Khayyám*   165

ALFRED, LORD TENNYSON, from "Crossing the Bar"   166

FRANCIS QUARLES, "A Good-Night"   166

SHAKESPEARE

  Song, from *Henry VIII*   167

  "Dirge," from *Cymbeline*   167

  from *The Tempest*   168

WILLIAM WORDSWORTH, from "Lines Composed a
  Few Miles Above Tintern Abbey"   169

JOHN KEATS, "On the Grasshopper and Cricket"   170

WALT WHITMAN, from "When lilacs last in the
  dooryard bloom'd"   171

ALGERNON CHARLES SWINBURNE, from "The Garden
  of Proserpine"   172

D. H. LAWRENCE, "Bavarian Gentians"   173

W. B. YEATS

    from "Fergus and the Druid"   174

JAMES LAUGHLIN, "Heart Island"   175

EUDORA WELTY, from *One Writer's Beginnings*   175

WENDELL BERRY, from "Poem for J."   176

GRETEL EHRLICH

    from *The Solace of Open Spaces*   176

JANE KENYON, "Let Evening Come"   177

ELIZABETH BISHOP, "One Art"   178

SAMUEL MENASHE, from "The Bare Tree"   179

JOHN ASHBERY, from "A Blessing in Disguise"   179

MURIEL RUKEYSER, from "The Sun-Artist"   180

WALLACE STEVENS, from "Peter Quince at the
  Clavier"   181

KEVIN PRUFER, "Returning to Friedrichskoog"   181

Healing, Changing, Moving On 183

GARY SNYDER 184

GEORGE HERBERT, from "The Flower" 185

SIR WALTER RALEGH, from "The Passionate Mans
 Pilgrimage" 185

JOHN MILTON, from "Lycidas" 186

MICHELANGELO BUONARROTI, "Dear to Me Is Sleep" 187

JAMES JOYCE, "Ecce Puer" 187

MARCEL PROUST, from *The Past Recaptured* 188

D. H. LAWRENCE, "Change" 189

Inscription on twelfth-century Egyptian stela 189

WALT WHITMAN, "The Last Invocation,"
 from *Leaves of Grass* 189

ABRAHAM LINCOLN 189

D. H. LAWRENCE, from "Ship of Death" 190

KAREN VERVAET, from "Karen's Journal" 191

SAMUEL MENASHE, "Promised Land" 192

HAROLD BRODKEY, from *This Wild Darkness* 192

STANLEY KUNITZ, from "The Layers" 195

FRANK O'HARA 196

JOHN BAYLEY, from *Elegy for Iris* 196

ANNA AKHMATOVA 197

W. S. MERWIN, from "Words for a Totem Animal" 197

MARK STRAND, "The End" 198

WENDELL BERRY, "A Man Walking and Singing" 199

ANNE SEXTON, "The Fury of Guitars and
 Sopranos" 202

SYLVIA PLATH, from "Berck-Plage" 203

CARL PHILLIPS, from "Cortège" 204

LOUISE BOGAN, "Song for the Last Act" 206

EUDORA WELTY, from *The Optimist's Daughter* 207

RAINIER MARIA RILKE   208

WILLIAM CARLOS WILLIAMS, "El Hombre"   209

ADRIENNE RICH, "Final Notations"   209

MARTHA WEINMAN LEAR, from *Heartsounds*   210

WALLACE STEVENS, "Of Mere Being"   210

From "Lord of the Dance" (folksong)   211

Suggested Readings for Friends and Family   213

Suggestions for Music   217

Index   223

Credits   243

Readings for Remembrance

Introduction

In a dark time, the best help is imagination—the mind lifted up like Noah's dove to wing its way to a restorative green tree. In that quest and to counter the isolation that can visit the bereaved in our society, I've brought together here examples of great and common literature to remind us all, myself included, that loss is the fundamental human experience, universally shared and collectively survived generation after generation. Indeed, the banality of death gave the worldly philosopher Montaigne reason to refuse to dread it, for "death mixes and confounds itself with all of our life . . . we must suffer patiently the laws of our being."

On the other hand, death is not so banal that the loss of a single loved person doesn't strike us with a shattering sense of unanticipated, never to be fully accepted, unreality. "I, Gilgamesh, king of Uruk, who slew Humbaba and the Bull of Heaven, fear death," comes the affrighted voice out of antiquity, spoken by the first humanized man-god in Western epic. The fear reverberates down time to the English Renaissance poet William Dunbar's *Timor Mortis conturbat me* (page 38) and Pascal's seventeenth-century *"le silence des espaces infinis m'effraye . . ."* In relatively modern times, Mark Twain, speaking of his daughter's death, said, "It is one of the mysteries of our nature that a man, all unprepared, can receive a thunderstroke like that and live."

And Ralph Waldo Emerson, after young Waldo's death, wrote, "Farewell and farewell . . . my darling my darling . . . my boy, my boy is gone . . . Shall I ever dare to love anything again?"

To one who receives such news, the world seems suddenly to drain of meaning. Then the standard literature of consolation of the past, full of piety and rhetoric, may seem vapid or maudlin, milking the hopelessness that is the human condition, affording little relief to those whose hearts are too full of pain to bear what is bogus. To turn again to Montaigne, speaker of things-as-they-are, in all the rest of life, "one can wear an actor's mask . . . but in that scene, there is no more feigning. We must speak," as he put it, "straightforward French."

What one craves at such a time is either plain speech or else cadences of scripture that drown personal grief in what Dylan Thomas called "the griefs of the ages." From friends one may even want a kind of bluntness, I think, rather than words of lying hope like Ezra Pound's, often quoted in such circumstances (page 155). For cruel truth says instead, "What thou lovest well" *has been* "reft from thee . . . ," and on that fact each person must build her or his philosophy of life and death.

A person can shape—and live by—a philosophy of life, but who can have a philosophy of death, if by "philosophy" we accept the dictionary definition of "a search for understanding"? For "death" as pure idea or concept bridges unbridgeable contradictions: a state of being and a state of non-being or *nothingness*. Now contradiction may be no stumbling block for a physicist exploring quantum theory and black holes by means of mathematical equations. But a mere language-speaker is hard put to span such a gap with ordinary reason.

Therefore, still in that spirit of quest, I propose to take a brief look at death apart from its meaning in experience, accepting that in its conceptual strangeness—which may have struck our ancestors even harder than it does ourselves—must lie the origin and function of our funeral and memorial services.

To begin, one can say plainly, "My friend is here no more," but the illogic of the statement is signalled by the words "is . . . no more." A classic way of dealing with contradiction was to keep a calm head and talk the matter over with plainspeaking friends. But twentieth-century postwar, postmodern thinkers provide no friendly help with their philosophies of nothingness. Heidegger proposed that dying was simply "not an event. It is a phenomenon to be understood existentially." Wittgenstein maintained death was beyond the power of the human mind to understand. For the social philosopher Philippe Ariès, death is only approachable through cultural practices it gives rise to. Simone Weil built an unstable definition on the paradox itself: "the dead have become something imaginary," she held. "The presence of the dead one is imaginary, but his absence is real, it is henceforth his manner of appearing."

If "death" is ungraspable as pure idea, so is its place in time between a past when the loved one was and a future when he or she never shall be more. But what is this Time that is continuous yet broken into two? Saint Augustine addressed his great meditations to the Timekeeper Himself: "Your years neither go nor come . . . they do not move on because they never pass at all. Your today is eternity . . . You made all time, you are before all time; and the 'time,' if such we may call it, when there was no time was not time at all." Albert Einstein might make peace with Time as a life-and-death enfolding totality (page 78), but in actuality, religious doctrines and the arts they generated leaned to one side or the other. That is to say, Egyptian death myth and icons focussed on the future life of the soul while Greek death images preserved idealized glimpses of the deceased's past. Today, traditional Christians and Muslims direct their prayers toward a supernatural future, while Jews mourn the historical past, and Hindus and Buddhists think of neither birth nor death as more than minor notches on the soul's wheel of Eternal Return. All the same, for many people now on earth, "real" psychological time may seem to stop like a clock when the death of a loved person is announced. Indeed, such moments pass in a timeless blur, a circumstance anthropologists call "liminal" or "beyond the threshold."

To accept such dissonance at the heart of our very sense of being, human societies have generated myths, art, and ritual ceremonies to insulate them against *timor mortis*. Prayers and rituals were once thought to purify the ground, the winds, and plants from malevolent spirits left in the wake of organic decay. Those fears are forgotten now, but a generalized sense that dangerous energies are loosed by one or multiple deaths resurges even in a technical-industrial world. Our funeral and memorial services, however plainspoken or elaborate they may be, still function to enclose the isolated, traumatized individual in the protective structures of society, which has survived burials without number. Indeed, these perhaps oldest of humanity's surviving "rites of passage" seem to have power to anneal even the alienated contemporary consciousness and to return it to the daylight world of time, action, and endurable emotion.

So the memorial service, with its panoply of readings and tender gestures, is a complex of survival instinct, cultural evolution, and esthetic imagination, choreographed over millennia by society's bereaved and their rabbis, priests, ministers, and advisers. The event might even be described as magical theater, promoting healing in the minds of a congregation. In this process, mourners' gestures and words, against a background of music, greenery, flowers, and such, serve as strategies of survival for individuals and their communities. And where official institutions like mainstream churches and temples fail to provide, people on their own will spontaneously invent collective rituals, as massive street events in London, New York, and elsewhere in the past few years have illustrated.

Communal mourning probably even helps restart a recuperative cycle. For what single mourner can help sooner or later becoming aware of the vast company she or he stands in, a company nearby and around the globe giving voice to perpetual lamentation? And so the personal gradually widens into the political, as feminists have been saying in other contexts for years now, and self-pity softens into compassion for humanity as a whole, which is fated by its physical and moral nature to suffer its losses. Ritualized mourning, even in secular terms, may insulate communities large and small against the kind of terrorized pessimism that, in some parts of the world, still ends in tragedy.

Some years ago, I attended a memorial service for an artist dead at a peaceful good age, but many of whose fellow artists had suffered suicidal anxiety and depression. In this case, there was the usual funeral home setup with podium, lectern, flowers, chairs, but here the event began even as people drifted to their seats. Nobody would have paid attention to the young man in blue jeans, who came out from a door behind the podium, if he hadn't been rolling a big truck tire that wobbled as he made his way to lean it against the back wall.

He left it there, went off, and came back with brushes and some jars of paint. He set them on the floor in front of the tire, spread out a newspaper, sat down with his back to the congregation. Then as most people went on talking among themselves quietly, he began laying thick, shiny strokes of color in spokes or rays around the flank of the tire. No one interrupted him or asked what he was doing, though no one seemed quite to understand. But when he was done and stood up, gathered his tools, and departed, we could see he had made out of practically nothing a most beautiful wreath of colors, a pure gift of imagination to the memory of an elder artist, Frederick Kiesler, from a younger, not yet so famous Robert Rauschenberg.

It was partly, I think, the *tactility* of that small act of dedication that has made me remember it so vividly. People want to touch or to witness touches of hands to the furniture of the ritual: artifacts, flowers, candles, a casket, the earth's good earth itself. I once dropped African daisies into a grave; another time, ashes into sand; yet again, ashes into the sea. I remember those moments and the three men they memorialize. Some people today leave stones on a grave; others, food and drink. Some leave gifts or letters. The grave is all that we have left of what was flesh and touchable. The pressure of hand on stone or wood calls to mind other touches, and so that small solemn act becomes a bridge between here and *nowhere*, but at least, *here*.

Watching the young Rauschenberg at work, I thought of the old tale of the *Jongleur de Notre-Dame*, the waif who had no coin to buy a gift for the Virgin on her special day, so he brought his juggling balls to church and performed at the foot of her statue, and was graciously smiled upon in return. I have a juggling ball of my own in this regard, which I lay at the metaphoric feet of the reader. I give you Nietzsche's idea that the most important thing for life and for death is "to obey at length and in a single direction," the course of one's destiny. "In the end, there results something for which it is worth the trouble of living on this earth, for example virtue, art, music, the dance, reason, the mind — something that transfigures, something delicate, mad or divine."

In a less personal sense, grandiose death rites further transfigure human beings who were, by their special destinies, already larger than life. Kings, emperors, queens, and film stars go to their graves with gun salutes, bagpipes, slow processionals, horses with reversed stirrups, black-hooded mourners. By these means, the mythologized dead are inserted into the flow of high history and, today, into the virtual reality of print and screen images in which our and our descendants' heads will no doubt swim. By these means, too, members of a national or cultural community are bonded so that, again, the single life rises out of isolation and, in a meltdown of social boundaries, takes on the glamour of the star. In our time, perhaps in all times, the boast, "I was there . . . ," has been a coded ticket of admission to a kind of immortality. In imagination, we live alongside the tombs of epic and poetry: barrows and pyres for fallen heroes. We join the processions and libations with feasting and gifts to the gods. How ancient is this matter of paying public honor to the dead! Indeed, according to Greek myth, a body lacking proper burial could not enter the underworld. Thus the hopeless fate of those fallen in foreign fields or into the sea.

On the fields of Marathon after the battle of 490 B.C.E., where a handful of Greeks decimated the hordes of the Persian king Darius the Great, a burial mound with ten name-bearing columns was raised soon after. It endured centuries and came to represent for the whole West the bitter value of heroism, of youthful self-sacrifice. I have included among the readings here excerpts from Pericles' famous address to the surviving Athenians (page 97), not for curiosity's sake but because by sharing such eulogies others may live their lives a little larger. Which is to remind us all, again, that we are not alone.

And thinking of Marathon and the name-bearing

columns—long since fallen—reminds me how the very form of memorial monuments has changed through time as have the rituals. From Ramses' obelisk to Titus's column to Napoleon's triumphal arch, and our own Washington Monument, the vertical, heaven-pointing shape evolved as religious ideas did. So today we have Maya Lin's conceptually revolutionary Vietnam Monument. Like the tumulus at Marathon, it bears the names of the dead, but on horizontal, polished walls that reflect back and forth the two worlds of here and nowhere, teaching this age of secular belief that the true afterlife is here among the faithful living, not in Valhalla with the gods.

To turn now to practical fact, funeral and memorial services have different functions and can be separated in time. The funeral takes place soon after a death, in certain communities within twenty-four hours and before sundown, and centers upon the casket or remains of the body. In this case, a religious spokesperson unfolds age-old litanies of tearing-away and relinquishing to ease this most painful of partings. A month, a season, or even a year later, a more or less secular service of remembrance may be offered by the family and friends.

All these services can take place in the spatial and doctrinal boundaries of a temple or church or else in a home or garden, on a hilltop or beach. But wherever the ceremony takes place, no moment in it is without significance. The processional or entry into a chapel or the stroll toward a garden, hilltop, or tree leads the mourners across that imaginary "threshold," away from habitual space-in-the-world into that unreal but vividly sensed "beyond." Indeed, any place on earth where the imagination conjures up honored or beloved ghosts can be, for people who visit it, so-called sacred space. So for the village burial ground, the small chapel, even, for a grieving family, a yard behind a house. Wherever it unfolds, the ceremony can include readings, music, eulogies, and small significant pantomimes perhaps involving water, flowers, greenery, spadefuls of earth, and so on. By these symbolic means, the message goes out that the circle has been pierced but not destroyed.

The selections that follow can be read aloud or in private, or lines might be singled out to help a speaker characterize the event in the imagery of high art. I made the selection trusting that most authentic art and literature are born in conscious or unconscious meditation on time and death. I could have filled a whole volume with John Donne or Wallace Stevens, D. H. Lawrence or Theodore Roethke, Emily Dickinson or Louise Bogan, but I've ranged much farther, passing over unbearable mourning cries like Antigone's over Oedipus, Medea's over her children, Electra's over Orestes, but including some scripture and hymns, some poems read aloud by generations, and examples from the classics arranged in rough chronological order. My modern/postmodern mind also craves today's language, spoken as if among friends, with mild irony and often a sense for the "nonprofessionalism" of the speaker. In a well-shaped service, a homegrown poet, a sensitive child, an ordinarily inarticulate relative can speak truth as Pound, in such a case, did not.

On the other hand, I realize it is the style sometimes nowadays to try to dispel gloom by telling funny stories about the deceased. Our society feels at ease in its worldly ethos, but I think a proper eulogy mixes lightness with references also to the deeper implications of the event. A photographer friend of mine has already planned her own service: "a slide show of my pictures, lots of chocolate, the twenty-third psalm sung by our mellifluous cantor, and a soprano sax solo by my son-in-law." Another friend wants music by the Tallis Scholars and Mozart's *Exsultate Jubilate* for her service. At a service I attended recently, friends evoked smiles for a man of vast wit while, alternately, his children spoke in another vein with unashamed tears. In the end, the congregation was moved, unconventionally, to applaud.

Unconventionally, because the memorial service is not a performance to be applauded but, again, a ritual with deep roots. The participants have come together not for entertainment but, whether they realize it or not, hoping to share in the psychic enlargement I've described. And, of course, for the family, the social act of structuring the service only begins a process of readaptation. In the end, as I've suggested, consolation comes with acceptance of our shared creaturehood.

I've divided the readings here into seven groups, loosely reflecting the movements of the memorial ceremony. The number seven itself is an ancient figure derived from the sun, moon, and the planets visible at night to the naked eye. I did not plan the book that way, but Dame Myth stepped in and led me.

The selections begin quietly, as if a grieving family or group of friends sat around talking, asking questions of one another about the purpose and form of their gathering. Not far beneath the surface, though, lie raw grief and even bitter anger, which can be echoed in the tropes of literature.

Along the way, the so-called Mysteries will be held up to, at best, a dim and shadowed light, and heroes and heroines of the past met as examples by which the deceased may be measured. For an ironic effect of our publicity-based culture is that a death can be quickly followed by professional or social oblivion, and a well-crafted memorial service can set an endangered reputation on a sound base in social memory, which is not to say that today's media stars bear comparison with Hercules or Beowulf.

Finally—to play one last time with paradox—finality is not an end much honored by postmodern writers and artists, who generally reject tidy wrap-ups as well as tragic epiphanies. "The poetry of earth is never dead," Keats wrote (page 170), and Roethke echoed, "What falls away is always. And is near." I conclude that we should not look for "closure" to our experiences of ultimate abandonment. To say it again, the memorial service only marks the start of a continuous process of survival lasting the rest of one's life.

Meanwhile, it was the depth of our grief that confirmed the depth of our love, and it was the love that blessed our lives.

Why We Gather

Every step and gesture of the funeral and memorial service is surrounded in mystery, and why human beings come together at all to mourn their dead is a deep unknown. We know only that, within the boundaries of the ceremony, we perform rituals as if to make each person's memory eternal. This practice, according to anthropological theory, began in ancient times to restore a sense of ongoing life to a bereaved community, to the individuals and families of which it is composed.

There be many shapes of mystery.
And many things God makes to be, past hope or fear,
And the end men looked for cometh not,
And a path is there where no one sought.
   So hath it fallen here.

EURIPIDES

Raphael, they're asking you to write a few lines
as an epitaph for the poet Ammonis:
something very tasteful and polished. You can do it,
you're the one to write something suitable
for the poet Ammonis, our Ammonis.

Of course you'll speak about his poems —
but say something too about his beauty,
about his subtle beauty that we loved.

Your Greek is always elegant and musical.
But we want all your craftsmanship now.
Our sorrow and our love move into a foreign
    language.
Pour your Egyptian feeling into the Greek you use.

Raphael, your verses, you know, should be written
so they contain something of our life within them,
so the rhythm, so every phrase clearly shows
that an Alexandrian is writing about an Alexandrian.

C. P. CAVAFY, "For Ammonis, Who Died at 29, in 610,"
translation by Edmund Keeley and Philip Sherrard

All you who mourn the loss of loved ones, and, at this
hour, remember the sweet companionship and the cher-
ished hopes that have passed away with them, give ear
to the word of comfort spoken in the name of God.
Only the body has died and has been laid in the dust.
The spirit lives in the shelter of God's love and mercy.
Our loved ones continue, also, in the remembrance of

those to whom they were precious. Their deeds of lovingkindness, the true and beautiful words they spoke
are treasured up as incentives to conduct by which the
living honor the dead. And when we ask in our grief:
Whence shall come our help and our comfort? then in
the strength of faith let us answer with the Psalmist:
My help cometh from God. He will not forsake us nor
leave us in our grief. Upon Him we cast our burden
and He will grant us strength according to the days He
has apportioned to us. All life comes from Him; all
souls are in His keeping. Come then, and in the midst
of sympathizing fellow-worshipers, rise and hallow the
name of God.

from a funeral service in
The Union Prayerbook

The late Marechal de Montluc told me how it broke his
heart that he had never allowed himself to be familiar
with his son—who died at Madeira, a youth of great
promise. By keeping up a stern paternal air, he said, he
lost his chance to know his son and let his own love be
known. . . .

I find this plaint well grounded, for experience has
taught me only too dearly that, in the loss of our
friends, there is no consolation so sweet as the knowledge that we had a perfect and complete understanding
with them, and had withheld from them nothing that
lay close to our heart. O my friend! am I better off or
worse for feeling that this was so with us? Surely I am

better off. I am consoled and honored by my grief. Is it not a pious and pleasing service in my life to be forever upon his funerals?

MICHEL DE MONTAIGNE,
from *The Autobiography*, translation
by Marvin Lowenthal

Who would not sing for Lycidas? He knew
Himself to sing, and build the lofty rhyme.
He must not float upon his wat'ry bier
Unwept, and welter to the parching wind,
Without the meed of some melodious tear.

JOHN MILTON, from "Lycidas"

They that mean to make no use of friends, will be at little trouble to gain them; and to be without friendship, is to be without one of the first comforts of our present state. To have no assistance from other minds, in resolving doubts, in appeasing scruples, in balancing deliberations, is a very wretched destitution. There is no wisdom in useless and hopeless sorrow, but there is something in it so like virtue, that he who is wholly without it cannot be loved, nor . . . be thought worthy of esteem. The loss of such a friend as has been taken from us increases our need of one another, and ought to unite us more closely.

SAMUEL JOHNSON, from *The Letters*

Márgarét, are you gríeving
Over Goldengrove unleaving?
Leáves, líke the things of man, you
With your fresh thoughts care for, can you?
Áh! ás the heart grows older
It will come to such sights colder
By and by, nor spare a sigh
Though worlds of wanwood leafmeal lie;
And yet you wíll weep and know why.
Now no matter, child, the name:
Sórrow's spríngs áre the same.
Nor mouth had, no nor mind, expressed
What heart heard of, ghost guessed:
It ís the blight man was born for,
It is Márgarét you mourn for.

GERARD MANLEY HOPKINS,

"Spring and Fall: To a Young Child"

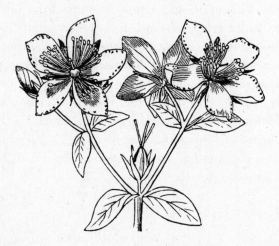

Emily Dickinson

There's a certain slant of light,
On winter afternoons,
That oppresses, like the weight
Of cathedral tunes.

Heavenly hurt it gives us;
We can find no scar,
But internal difference
Where the meanings are.

None may teach it anything,
'T is the seal, despair, —
An imperial affliction
Sent us of the air.

When it comes, the landscape listens,
Shadows hold their breath;
When it goes, 't is like the distance
On the look of death.

"There's a certain slant of light"

The bustle in a house
The morning after death
Is solemnest of industries
Enacted upon earth, —

The sweeping up the heart,
And putting love away
We shall not want to use again
Until eternity.

"The bustle in a house"

❧

[Man] does not live by care for himself, but by love for others. It was not given the mother to know what was necessary for the life of her children; it was not given to the rich man to know what was necessary for himself. . . . The orphans lived not by any care they had for themselves, they lived through the love that was in the heart of a stranger . . . and all people live, not by reason of any care they have for themselves, but by the love for them that is in other people. . . . God does not desire human beings to live apart from one another, and therefore has not revealed to them what is necessary for each to live alone. He wishes them to live together united, and therefore has revealed to them that they are necessary to each other's happiness.

LEO TOLSTOY, from What Men Live By

So, we'll go no more a-roving
   So late into the night,
Though the heart be still as loving,
   And the moon be still as bright.

For the sword outwears its sheath,
    And the soul wears out the breast,
And the heart must pause to breathe,
    And Love itself have rest.

Though the night was made for loving,
    And the day returns too soon,
Yet we'll go no more a-roving
    By the light of the moon.

GEORGE GORDON, LORD BYRON,
    "So, We'll Go No More A-Roving"

We'll to the woods no more,
The laurels all are cut,
The bowers are bare of bay
That once the Muses wore;
The year draws in the day
And soon will evening shut:
The laurels all are cut,
We'll to the woods no more.
Oh we'll no more, no more
To the leafy woods away,
To the high wild woods of laurel
And the bowers of bay no more.

A. E. HOUSMAN, "We'll to the Woods No More"

No more walks in the wood:
The trees have all been cut
Down, and where once they stood

Not even a wagon rut
Appears along the path
Low brush is taking over

No more walks in the wood;
This is the aftermath
Of afternoons in the clover
Fields where we once made love
Then wandered home together
Where the trees arched above,
Where we made our own weather
When branches were the sky.
Now they are gone for good,
And you, for ill, and I
Am only a passer-by.

We and the trees and the way
Back from the fields of play
Lasted as long as we could.
No more walks in the wood.

JOHN HOLLANDER, "An Old-Fashioned Song"
("Nous n'irons plus au bois")

Wednesday, 3rd September. Coleridge, Wm., and John
went from home, to go upon Helvellyn with Mr. Simpson. They set out after breakfast. I accompanied them
up near the blacksmith's. . . . I then went to a funeral at
John Dawson's. About 10 men and 4 women. Bread,
cheese, and ale. They talked sensibly and cheerfully
about common things. The dead person, 56 years of
age, buried by the parish. The coffin was neatly lettered

and painted black, and covered with a decent cloth. They set the corpse down at the door; and, while we stood within the threshold, the men with their hats off sang with decent and solemn countenances a verse of a funeral psalm. The corpse was then borne down the hill, and they sang till they had passed the Town-End. I was affected to tears while we stood in the house, the coffin lying before me. There were no near kindred, no children. When we got out of the dark house the sun was shining, and the prospect looked as divinely beautiful as I ever saw it. It seemed more sacred than I had ever seen it, and yet more allied to human life. The green fields, neighbours of the churchyard, were as green as possible; and, with the brightness of the sunshine, looked quite gay. I thought she was going to a quiet spot, and I could not help weeping very much. When we came to the bridge, they began to sing again, and stopped during four lines before they entered the churchyard. . . . Wm. and John came home at 10 o'clock.

DOROTHY WORDSWORTH, from the *Journal*

This is thy hour O Soul, thy free flight into the
    wordless,
Away from books, away from art, the day erased, the
    lesson done,
Thee fully forth emerging, silent, gazing,
    pondering the themes thou lovest best,
Night, sleep, death and the stars.

WALT WHITMAN, from "A Clear Midnight"

I strove with none, for none was worth my strife.
Nature I loved and, next to Nature, Art:
I warm'd both hands before the fire of life;
It sinks, and I am ready to depart.

WALTER SAVAGE LANDOR, "Finis"

Li Po

The moon above the palace of Han
  And above the land of Chin,
Shedding a flood of silvery light,
  Bids the radiant lady farewell.
She sets out on the road of the Jewel Gate—
  The road she will not travel back.
The moon returns above the palace of Han,
  Rising from the eastern seas,
But the radiant lady wed in the west,
  She will return nevermore.
On the Mongolian mountains flowers are made
  Of the long winter's snow.
The moth-eyebrowed one, broken-hearted,
  Lies buried in the desert sand.
Living, she lacked the gold,
  And her portrait was distorted;
Dying she leaves a green mound,
  Which moves all the world to pity.

"Lady Wang-Chao—II"

My friend bade farewell at the Yellow Crane House,
And went down eastward to Willow Valley
Amid the flowers and mists of March.
The lonely sail in the distance
Vanished at last beyond the blue sky.
And I could see only the river
Flowing along the border of heaven.

"On Seeing Off Meng Hao-Jan"

Prairie
is the best soil for burial,
an acre or two away from town.

There's no silence here not crowded
with the sound of bees,
cicadas, meadowlarks in summer
and all year 'round the many-voiced wind.

Listen, how it jostles
the elbows of the corn akimbo.
It blows through the long-needled pines
like the ghost of a child piping
with paper and comb.

At the iron fence it pauses,
lightly ruffling the wild roses by the gate.
You can barely feel it move
as it slips between the granite headstones
carved with the names of grandparents,
parents, uncles, aunts.

All children return to this place,
faithful and prodigal alike.
In this acre they're forgiven everything.
And the meadowlark, who knows nothing of death,
sings his song as sweetly for them
as he will for us.

CONSTANCE EGEMO, "The Gathering"

We buried him with simplicity as Jewish law makes it easy to do. Though he himself might have preferred a Mass in a cathedral with Baroque music pouring down from the galleries, or a funeral like the one a friend arranged for his mother in Venice, with black-draped gondolas gliding out to the Isle of the Dead, he lies in the place of places I would have chosen for him. It is a small, walled-in field with ragged pines and poppies sown through uncut grass. At the time it seemed to me a place oddly my own, though I didn't understand why. I only knew the privacy and sweet fragrance, common colors and grey stone of a few leaning markers made a scene I remembered with a sense of fitness. Later, of course, I realized the image of the meadow served to bind him at the end into the form of my life instead of my being displaced into his, which had been the usual style of our life together.

E. M., from *Memoir of*
a Modernist's Daughter

There it was, on a little river island, that once, whether sleeping or waking we know not, we saw celebrated a Fairy's Funeral. First we heard small pipes playing as if no bigger than hollow rushes that whisper to the night winds; and more piteous than aught that trills from earthly instrument was the scarce audible dirge. It seemed to float over the stream, every foam-bell emitting a plaintive note, till the airy anthem came floating over our couch, and then alighted without footsteps among the heather. The pattering of little feet was then heard as if living creatures were arranging themselves

in order, and then there was nothing but a more or-
dered hymn. The harmony was like the melting of musical dewdrops, and sung, without words, of sorrow
and death. We opened our eyes: or rather, sight came to
them when closed, and dream was vision. Hundreds of
creatures no taller than the crest of the lapwing, and all
hanging down their veiled heads, stood in a circle on a
green plot among the rocks; and in the midst was a bier,
framed, as it seemed, of flowers unknown among the
Highland hills; and on the bier a Fairy lying with uncovered face, pale as the lily, motionless as the snow.
The dirge grew fainter and fainter, and then died quite
away; when two of the creatures came from the circle
and took their station, one at the head and the other at
the foot of the bier. They sang alternate measures, not
louder than the twittering of the awakened wood-lark
before it goes up the dewy air, but dolorous and full of
the desolation of death. The flower-bier stirred; for the
spot on which it lay sank slowly down, and in a few
moments the greensward was smooth as ever—the very
dews glittering above the buried Fairy. A cloud passed
over the moon, and, with a choral lament, the funeral
troop sailed duskily away, heard afar off, so still was
the midnight solitude of the glen.

CHRISTOPHER NORTH (JOHN WILSON),

from "A Fairy's Funeral"

[L]et's bless the imagination. It gives
us the myths we live by. Let's bless
the visionary power of the human—
the only animal that's got it—,

bless the exact image of your father
dead and mine dead, bless the images
that stalk the corners of our sight
and will not let go.

PHILIP LEVINE, from "On the Meeting of
García Lorca and Hart Crane"

However much we are affected by the things of the
world, however deeply they may stir and stimulate us,
they become human for us only when we can discuss
them with our fellows. . . . We humanize what is going
on in the world and in ourselves only by speaking of it,
and in the course of speaking of it, we learn to be
human.

HANNAH ARENDT

I will teach you my townspeople
how to perform a funeral
for you have it over a troop
of artists—
unless one should scour the world—
you have the ground sense necessary.

See! the hearse leads.
I begin with a design for a hearse.
For Christ's sake not black—
nor white either—and not polished!
Let it be weathered—like a farm wagon—
with gilt wheels (this could be
applied fresh at small expense)

or no wheels at all:
a rough dray to drag over the ground.

Knock the glass out!
My God—glass, my townspeople!
For what purpose? Is it for the dead
to look out or for us to see
how well he is housed or to see
the flowers or the lack of them—
or what?
To keep the rain and snow from him?
He will have a heavier rain soon:
pebbles and dirt and what not.
Let there be no glass—
and no upholstery, phew!
and no little brass rollers
and small easy wheels on the bottom—
my townspeople what are you thinking of?

A rough plain hearse then
with gilt wheels and no top at all.
On this the coffin lies
by its own weight.

        No wreaths please—
especially no hot house flowers.
Some common memento is better,
something he prized and is known by:
his old clothes—a few books perhaps—
God knows what! You realize
how we are about these things
my townspeople—

something will be found—anything
even flowers if he had come to that.
So much for the hearse.

For heaven's sake though see to the driver!
Take off the silk hat! In fact
that's no place at all for him—
up there unceremoniously
dragging our friend out to his own dignity!
Bring him down—bring him down!
Low and inconspicuous! I'd not have him ride
on the wagon at all—damn him—
the undertaker's understrapper!
Let him hold the reins
and walk at the side
and inconspicuously too!

Then briefly as to yourselves:
Walk behind—as they do in France,
seventh class, or if you ride
Hell take curtains! Go with some show
of inconvenience; sit openly—
to the weather as to grief.
Or do you think you can shut grief in?
What—from us? We who have perhaps
nothing to lose? Share with us
share with us—it will be money
in your pockets.

Go now
I think you are ready.

WILLIAM CARLOS WILLIAMS, "Tract"

While the earth turns,
And the skin of it — O, scientist —
Keeps cool, keeps deep;

While the world shines,
And the rind of it — O, radium —
Still does not burn;

While — but why wait?
Don't you hear the dance music,
Old as these hills?

Round with it, round with it,
Stepping, oh, ever so lightly,
Wind in the hair —

What now? You have stopped,
You are weeping. Well, it is difficult,
Dear ones. It is.

MARK VAN DOREN, "What Now?"

Raw Grief and
Bitter Mourning

The fabric of individual and community life is torn. Whether in the fullness of time or by sudden catastrophe, the deceased is mourned at first with overwhelming emotion. The funeral and memorial service help to contain these often unbearable feelings in the context of shared human experience.

[I]t was my heartache for you, my Odysseus, and for your wise and gentle ways, that brought my life and all its sweetness to an end.

HOMER, from *The Odyssey* (Book II)

Over many lands and seas have I journeyed, brother, to add my tears to the silent ashes on your tomb. Since destiny has carried you off before your time, poor brother, it falls to me to perform the old, sad rite. Receive it and with it, my tears of love and grief.

And so forever, brother, hail and farewell!

CATULLUS

Melpomene, teach me how to grieve,
you to whom your father gave the lyre
and your tremulous voice!
And so will Quintilius never wake again, never?
    Then where will Honor, Faith and simple Truth find his equal?

HORACE

God of pity and love, return to this earth.
Go not so far away, leaving us to evil.
Return, oh Lord, return. Come with the day.
Come with the light, that men may see once more
Across this earth's uncomfortable floor
The kindly path, the old and living way.
Let us not die of evil in the night.
Let there be God again. Let there be light.

from the Yom Kippur morning service in
The Union Prayerbook

Saint Augustine, from The Confessions

On the ninth day of her sickness, and the fifty-sixth year of her age, and the three and thirtieth of mine, was that religious and holy soul freed from the body.

I closed her eyes; and there flowed a mighty sorrow into my heart, which was overflowing into tears; mine eyes at the same time, by the violent command of my mind, drank up their fountain wholly dry; and woe was me in such a strife! But when she breathed her last, . . . a childish feeling in me, which was, through my heart's youthful voice, finding its vent in weeping, was checked and silenced. For we thought it not fitting to solemnize that funeral with tearful lament, and groanings: for thereby do they for the most part express grief for the departed, as though unhappy, or altogether dead; whereas she was neither unhappy in her death, nor altogether dead. Of this, we were assured on good grounds, the testimony of her good conversation and her *faith unfeigned*.

What then was it which did grievously pain me within, but a fresh wound wrought through the sudden wrench of that most sweet and dear custom of living together? Being then forsaken of so great comfort in her, my soul was wounded, and that life rent asunder as it were, which, of hers and mine together, had been made but one. . . .

I blamed the weakness of my feelings, and refrained my flood of grief, which gave way a little unto me; but again came, as with a tide, yet not so as to burst out into tears, nor to a change of countenance; still I knew what I was keeping down in my heart. And . . . with a new grief I grieved for my grief, and was thus worn by a double sorrow.

And behold, the corpse was carried to the burial; we went and returned without tears. . . .

And then, little by little, I gave way to the tears which I before restrained, to overflow as much as they desired; reposing my heart upon them; and it found rest in them, for it was in Thy ears, not in those of man, who would have scornfully interpreted my weeping. And now, Lord, in writing I confess it unto Thee. Read it, who will, and interpret it, how he will: and if he finds sin therein, that I wept my mother for a small portion of an hour, (the mother who for the time was dead to mine eyes, who had for many years wept for me, that I might live in Thine eyes,) let him not deride me; but rather, if he be one of large charity, let him weep himself for my sins unto Thee.

from "On the Death of His Mother"

I had one friend, too dear to me, from a community of pursuits, of mine own age and, as myself, in the first opening flower of youth. He had grown up of a child with me, and we had been both school-fellows and playfellows. . . .

Thou tookest that man out of this life, when he had scarce filled up one whole year of my friendship, sweet to me above all sweetness of that my life. . . .

At this grief my heart was utterly darkened, and whatever I beheld was death. My native country was a torment to me, and my father's house a strange unhappiness; and whatever I had shared with him, wanting him, became a distracting torture. Mine eyes sought him every where, but he was not granted them; and I hated all places, for that they had not him; nor could they now tell me, "he is coming," as when he was alive and absent. I became a great riddle to myself, and I asked my soul, *why she was so sad, and why she disquieted me sorely:* but she knew not what to answer me. And if I said, *Trust in God,* she very rightly obeyed me not; because that most dear friend, whom she had lost, was, being man, both truer and better, than that phantasm she was bid to trust in. Only tears were sweet to me, for they succeeded my friend, in the dearest of my affections.

from "On the Death of a Friend"

I that in heill was and gladness
Am trublit now with great sickness
And feblit with infirmitie:—
    Timor Mortis conturbat me.

Our plesance here is all vain glory,
This fals world is but transitory,
The flesh is bruckle, the Feynd is slee:—
    Timor Mortis conturbat me.

The state of man does change and vary,
Now sound, now sick, now blyth, now sary,
Now dansand mirry, now like to die:—
Timor Mortis conturbat me.

Sen he has all my brether tane,
He will naught let me live alane;
Of force I man his next prey be:—
Timor Mortis conturbat me.

Since for the Death remeid is none,
Best is that we for Death dispone,
After our death that live may we:—
Timor Mortis conturbat me.

WILLIAM DUNBAR,
from "Lament for the Makers"

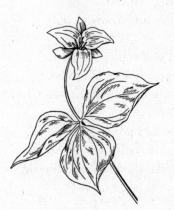

John Clare

Wilt thou go with me, sweet maid,
Say, maiden, wilt thou go with me
Through the valley-depths of shade,
Of night and dark obscurity;

Where the path has lost its way,
Where the sun forgets the day,
Where there's nor life nor light to see,
Sweet maiden, wilt thou go with me?

Where stones will turn to flooding streams,
Where plains will rise like ocean waves,
Where life will fade like visioned dreams
And mountains darken into caves,
Say, maiden, wilt thou go with me
Through this sad non-identity,
Where parents live and are forgot,
And sisters live and know us not?

Say, maiden, wilt thou go with me
In this strange death of life to be,
To live in death and be the same,
Without this life or home or name,
At once to be and not to be —
That was and is not — yet to see
Things pass like shadows, and the sky
Above, below, around us lie?

The land of shadows wilt thou trace,
And look — nor know each other's face;

The present mixed with reason gone,
And past and present all as one?
Say, maiden, can thy life be led
To join the living with the dead?
Then trace thy footsteps on with me;
We're wed to one eternity.

"An Invite, to Eternity"

I am — yet what I am none cares or knows,
    My friends forsake me like a memory lost;
I am the self-consumer of my woes,
    They rise and vanish in oblivions host,
Like shadows in love — frenzied stifled throes
And yet I am, and live like vapours tost

Into the nothingness of scorn and noise,
    Into the living sea of waking dreams,
Where there is neither sense of life or joys,
    But the vast shipwreck of my life's esteems;
And e'en the dearest — that I love the best —
Are strange — nay, rather stranger than the rest.

I long for scenes where man has never trod,
    A place where woman never smiled or wept;
There to abide with my Creator, God,
    And sleep as I in childhood sweetly slept;
Untroubling and untroubled where I lie,
The grass below — above the vaulted sky.

"I Am"

Ben Jonson

Slow, slow, fresh fount, keep time with my salt tears;
   Yet slower yet, oh faintly, gentle springs;
List to the heavy part the music bears,
   Woe weeps out her division when she sings.
      Droop herbs and flowers,
      Fall grief in showers;
      Our beauties are not ours;
       Oh, I could still,
Like melting snow upon some craggy hill,
   Drop, drop, drop, drop,
Since nature's pride is now a withered daffodil.

from "Cynthia's Reve"

Farewell, thou child of my right hand, and joy;
   My sin was too much hope of thee, loved boy.
Seven years thou wert lent to me, and I thee pay,
   Exacted by thy fate, on the just day.
Oh, could I lose all father now! For why
   Will man lament the state he should envy?
To have so soon 'scaped world's and flesh's rage,
   And if no other misery, yet age!
Rest in soft peace, and asked, say, Here doth lie
   Ben Jonson his best piece of poetry.
For whose sake henceforth all his vows be such
   As what he loves may never like too much.

"On my first son"

❧

Farewell dear babe, my heart's too much content,
Farewell sweet babe, the pleasure of mine eye,
Farewell fair flower that for a space was lent,
Then ta'en away unto eternity.
Blest babe, why should I once bewail thy fate,
Or sigh thy days so soon were terminate,
Sith thou art settled in an everlasting state.

> ANNE BRADSTREET, from "In Memory of My Dear
> Grandchild Elizabeth Bradstreet, Who Deceased
> August, 1665, Being a Year and Half Old"

I have suffered more than ever I thought I could have
done for a child still born. . . . I refused to see the little
body at first, . . . but he looked (if it be not absurd to
call a newborn babe so) even majestic in his mysterious
silence after all the turmoil of the night before.

> ALFRED, LORD TENNYSON

Dream that my little baby came to life again; that it had
only been cold, and that we rubbed it before the fire,
and it lived. Awake and find no baby. I think about the
little thing all day. Not in good spirits.

> MARY WOLLSTONECRAFT

Here lies, but seven years old, our little maid,
Once of the darkness, oh, so sore afraid,
Light of the World—remember that small fear,
And when nor moon nor stars do shine—draw near!

> WALTER DE LA MARE, "Even in the Grave"

The South-wind brings
Life, sunshine and desire,
And on every mount and meadow
Breathes aromatic fire;
But over the dead he has no power,
The lost, the lost, he cannot restore;
And, looking over the hills, I mourn
The darling who shall not return.

I see my empty house,
I see my trees repair their boughs;
And he, the wondrous child,
Whose silver warble wild
Outvalued every pulsing sound
Within the air's cerulean round,—
The hyacinthine boy, for whom
Morn well might break and April bloom,—
The gracious boy, who did adorn
The world whereinto he was born,
And by his countenance repay
The favor of the loving Day,—
Has disappeared from the Day's eye;
Far and wide she cannot find him;
My hopes pursue, they cannot bind him.
Returned this day, the south wind searches,
And finds young pines and budding birches;
But finds not the budding man;
Nature, who lost, cannot remake him;
Fate let him fall, Fate can't retake him;
Nature, Fate, men, him seek in vain.

And whither now, my truant wise and sweet,
O, whither tend thy feet?
I had the right, few days ago,
Thy steps to watch, thy place to know:
How have I forfeited the right?
Hast thou forgot me in a new delight?
I hearken for thy household cheer,
O eloquent child!

. . .

O child of paradise,
Boy who made dear his father's home,
In whose deep eyes
Men read the welfare of the times to come,
I am too much bereft.
The world dishonored thou hast left.
O truth's and nature's costly lie!
O trusted broken prophecy!
O richest fortune sourly crossed!
Born for the future, to the future lost!

> RALPH WALDO EMERSON, from "Threnody"

I weep for Adonais—he is dead!
O, weep for Adonais! though our tears
Thaw not the frost which binds so dear a head!
And thou, sad Hour, selected from all years
To mourn our loss, rouse thy obscure compeers,
And teach them thine own sorrow, say: "With me
Died Adonais; till the Future dares
Forget the Past, his fate and fame shall be
An echo and a light unto eternity!"

. . .

Oh, weep for Adonais—he is dead!
Wake, melancholy Mother, wake and weep!
Yet wherefore? Quench within their burning bed
Thy fiery tears, and let thy loud heart keep
Like his, a mute and uncomplaining sleep;
For he is gone, where all things wise and fair
Descend;—oh, dream not that the amorous Deep
Will yet restore him to the vital air;
Death feeds on his mute voice, and laughs at our
    despair.

PERCY BYSSHE SHELLEY,
from "Adonais: An Elegy on the
Death of John Keats"

There is nothing more terrible than the recent death
of one beloved. During the forty-nine days of ritual ob-
servance and the retreat to a mountain temple with
other mourners, every fibre of emotion is wrung when
in these narrow and solitary surroundings are celebrated the masses for the dead. Yet those days glide
swiftly away and, on the last, desolation is again our
portion as we collect our belongings and disperse
silently on our several ways to return to the saddened
house.

We do not willingly forget the beloved, but days go
by and, as says the proverb, "Those departed become
strangers and remote." The shock subsides. We must
laugh and be trivial. The body is buried on a lonely and
far-off mountain, and is visited only on ritual days. Before long the sotoba [memorial stone] is overgrown

with moss and heaped with dead leaves, and the only faithful visitors are the night-wind and the moon. Though for the newly dead many sorrow, who values the long departed? Posterity for awhile may know the name of the ancestor, for that is a handed-down tradition, but what grief can they feel? No longer are offerings made or any services of remembrance held, and gradually the name itself is forgotten and none know who lies in the nameless grave. The grass in spring overgrowing it may rouse some emotion. It may be sad to hear that the ancient pine-tree of a thousand years has fallen in a great storm and is now cut up for firewood. And then the ancient graveyard becomes a ploughed field, and its place knows it no more. Such is the pity of things!

ANONYMOUS, translation from the Japanese
by Ryukichi Kurata

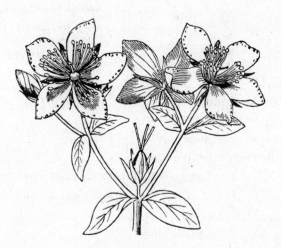

Japanese Poems

Long, long since I saw the building of my beloved's
   house.
Now it is desolate.
The roof and the fence have fallen, and only the violets
Still blossom in deep grass.

EMPEROR HORIKAWA,
translation from the Japanese
by Ryukichi Kurata

The servants, the pomp, have vanished, and I am no
   more courted.
Forgotten and lonely my palace, for all are seeking the
   new one.
Unswept the flowers lie in the sad untended garden.

EMPEROR HANAZONO,
translation from the Japanese
by Ryukichi Kurata

LXXIX
In all the world
There is no way whatever.
The stag cries even
In the most remote mountain.

THE PRIEST FUJIWARA NO TOSHINARI,
translation by Kenneth Rexroth

XCVIII

We were together
Only a little while,
And we believed our love
Would last a thousand years.

YAKAMOCHI, translation by Kenneth Rexroth

V

The mists rise over
The still pools at Asuka.
Memory does not
Pass away so easily.

AKAHITO, translation by Kenneth Rexroth

XCIX

Others may forget you, but not I.
I am haunted by your beautiful ghost.

THE EMPRESS YAMATOHIME,
translation by Kenneth Rexroth

Gerard Manley Hopkins

No worst, there is none. Pitched past pitch of grief,
More pangs will, schooled at forepangs, wilder wring.
Comforter, where, where is your comforting?
Mary, mother of us, where is your relief?
  . . .

   O the mind, mind has mountains; cliffs of fall
Frightful, sheer, no-man-fathomed. Hold them cheap
May who ne'er hung there. Nor does long our small
Durance deal with that steep or deep. Here! creep,
Wretch, under a comfort serves in a whirlwind: all
Life death does end and each day dies with sleep.

from "No worst, there is none"

I wake and feel the fell of dark, not day.
What hours, O what black hours we have spent
This night! what sights you, heart, saw; ways you
    went!
And more must, in yet longer light's delay.
   With witness I speak this. But where I say
Hours I mean years, mean life. And my lament
Is cries countless, cries like dead letters sent
To dearest him that lives alas! away.
  . . .

The lost are like this, and their scourge to be
As I am mine, their sweating selves; but worse.

from "I wake and feel the fell of dark"

After great pain, a formal feeling comes—
The Nerves sit ceremonious, like Tombs—
The stiff Heart questions—was it He, that bore,
And Yesterday, or Centuries before?

The Feet, mechanical, go round—
Of Ground, or Air, or Ought—
A Wooden way
Regardless grown,
A Quartz contentment, like a stone—

This is the Hour of Lead—
Remembered, if outlived,
As Freezing persons, recollect the Snow—
First—Chill—then Stupor—then the letting go—

EMILY DICKINSON, "After great pain"

Down west, down west we dance,
We spirits dance,
We spirits weeping dance.

WINTU, "We Spirits Dance"

James Joyce

Gabriel, leaning on his elbow, looked for a few moments unresentfully on her tangled hair and half-open mouth, listening to her deep-drawn breath. . . .

The air of the room chilled his shoulders. He stretched himself cautiously along under the sheets and lay down beside his wife. One by one, they were all becoming shades. Better pass boldly into that other world, in the full glory of some passion, than fade and wither dismally with age. He thought of how she who lay beside him had locked in her heart for so many years that image of her lover's eyes when he had told her that he did not wish to live.

Generous tears filled Gabriel's eyes. He had never felt like that himself towards any woman, but he knew that such a feeling must be love. The tears gathered more thickly in his eyes and in the partial darkness he imagined he saw the form of a young man standing under a dripping tree. Other forms were near. His soul had approached that region where dwell the vast hosts of the dead. He was conscious of, but could not apprehend, their wayward and flickering existence. His own identity was fading out into a grey impalpable world: the solid world itself, which these dead had one time reared and lived in, was dissolving and dwindling.

A few light taps upon the pane made him turn to the window. It had begun to snow again. He watched sleepily the flakes, silver and dark, falling obliquely against the lamplight. The time had come for him to set out on his journey westward. Yes, the newspapers were right: snow was general all over Ireland. It was falling on every part of the dark central plain, on the treeless hills, falling softly upon the Bog of Allen and, farther westward, softly falling into the dark mutinous Shannon waves. It was falling, too, upon every part of the lonely churchyard on the hill where Michael Furey lay buried. It lay thickly drifted on the crooked crosses and headstones, on the spears of the little gate, on the barren thorns. His soul swooned slowly as he heard the snow falling faintly through the universe and faintly falling, like the descent of their last end, upon all the living and the dead.

from "The Dead"

And it's old and old it's sad and old it's sad and weary I go back to you, my cold father, my cold, mad father, my cold mad feary father, till the near sight of the mere size of him, the moyles and moyles of it, moananoaning, makes me seasilt saltsick and I rush, my only, into your arms . . .

from *Finnegans Wake*

Can I see another's woe
And not be in sorrow too?
Can I see another's grief
And not seek for kind relief?

Can I see a falling tear
And not feel my sorrow's share?
Can a father see his child
Weep, nor be with sorrow fill'd?

Can a mother sit and hear
An infant groan an infant fear?
No, no! never can it be!
Never, never can it be!

And can he who smiles on all
Hear the wren with sorrows small,
Hear the small bird's grief & care,
Hear the woes that infants bear,

And not sit beside the nest
Pouring pity in their breast;
And not sit the cradle near
Weeping tear on infant's tear;

And not sit both night & day
Wiping all our tears away?
O! no never can it be!
Never, never can it be!

He doth give his joy to all;
He becomes an infant small;
He becomes a man of woe;
He doth feel the sorrow too.

Think not thou canst sigh a sigh
And thy maker is not by;
Think not thou canst weep a tear
And thy maker is not near.

O! he gives to us his joy
That our grief he may destroy;
Till our grief is fled & gone
He doth sit by us and moan.

WILLIAM BLAKE, "On Another's Sorrow"

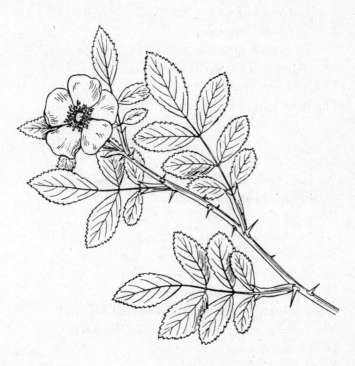

Thomas Hardy

You did not walk with me
Of late to the hill-top tree
   By the gated ways
   As in earlier days
. . .
I went alone, and I did not mind,
Not thinking of you as left behind.

I walked up there to-day
Just in the former way;
   Surveyed around
   The familiar ground
   By myself again:
   What difference, then?
Only that underlying sense
Of the look of a room on returning thence.

from "The Walk"

Woman much missed, how you call to me, call to me,
Saying that now you are not as you were
When you had changed
   from the one who was all to me,
But as at first, when our day was fair.

Or is it only the breeze, in its listlessness
Travelling across the wet mead to me here,
You being ever dissolved to wan wistlessness,
Heard no more again far or near?

Thus I; faltering forward,
　　Leaves around me falling,
Wind oozing thin through the thorn from norward,
　　And the woman calling.

from "The Voice"

The night has a thousand eyes.
　　And the day but one;
Yet the light of the bright world dies
　　With the dying sun

The mind has a thousand eyes.
　　And the heart but one;
Yet the light of a whole life dies
　　When love is done.

FRANCIS WILLIAM BOURDILLON, "Light"

Stop all the clocks, cut off the telephone,
Prevent the dog from barking with a juicy bone,
Silence the pianos and with muffled drum
Bring out the coffin, let the mourners come.

Let aeroplanes circle moaning overhead
Scribbling on the sky the message He Is Dead,
Put crêpe bows round the white necks of the public
　　doves,
Let the traffic policemen wear black cotton gloves.

He was my North, my South, my East and West,
My working week and my Sunday rest,
My noon, my midnight, my talk, my song;
I thought that love would last for ever: I was wrong.

The stars are not wanted now: put out every one;
Pack up the moon and dismantle the sun;
Pour away the ocean and sweep up the wood;
For nothing now can ever come to any good.

W. H. AUDEN, "Funeral Blues"

What passing-bells for these who die as cattle?
  —Only the monstrous anger of the guns.
  Only the stuttering rifles' rapid rattle
Can patter out their hasty orisons.
No mockeries now for them; no prayers nor bells;
  Nor any voice of mourning save the choirs,—
The shrill, demented choirs of wailing shells;
  And bugles calling for them from sad shires.

What candles may be held to speed them all?
  Not in the hands of boys but in their eyes
Shall shine the holy glimmers of goodbyes.
  The pallor of girls' brows shall be their pall;
Their flowers the tenderness of patient minds,
And each slow dusk a drawing-down of blinds.

WILFRED OWEN, "Anthem for Doomed Youth"

After the planes unloaded, we fell down
Buried together, unmarried men and women;

Not crown of thorns, not iron, not Lombard crown,
Not grilled and spindle spires pointing to heaven
Could save us. Raise us, Mother, we fell down
Here hugger-mugger in the jellied fire:
Our sacred earth in our day was our curse.

Our Mother, shall we rise on Mary's day
In Maryland, wherever corpses married
Under the rubble, bundled together? Pray
For us whom the blockbusters marred and buried;
When Satan scatters us on Rising-day,
O Mother, snatch our bodies from the fire:
Our sacred earth in our day was our curse.

Mother, my bones are trembling and I hear
The earth's reverberations and the trumpet
Bleating into my shambles. Shall I bear,
(O Mary!) unmarried man and powder-puppet,
Witness to the Devil? Mary, hear,
O Mary, marry earth, sea, air and fire;
Our sacred earth in our day is our curse.

ROBERT LOWELL, "The Dead in Europe"

Black milk of daybreak we drink you at night
we drink in the morning at noon we drink you at
   sundown
we drink and we drink you
A man lives in the house he plays with the serpents he
   writes
he writes when dusk falls to Germany your golden
   hair Margarete

your ashen hair Shulamith we dig a grave in the
 breezes there one lies unconfined
. . .

Black milk of daybreak we drink you at night
we drink you at noon in the morning we drink you at
 sundown
we drink and we drink you
a man lives in the house your golden hair Margarete
your ashen hair Shulamith he plays with the serpents

He calls out more sweetly play death death is a master
 from Germany
he calls out more darkly now stroke your strings then
 as smoke you will rise into air
then a grave you will have in the clouds there one lies
 unconfined
. . .

your golden hair Margarete
your ashen hair Shulamith

PAUL CELAN, from "Death Fugue,"
translation by Michael Hamburger

You lie there, Anna,
In your grave now,
Under a snow-sky,
You lie there now.

Where have the dead gone?
Where do they live now?
Not in the grave, they say,
Then where now?

Tell me, tell me,
Is it where I may go?
Ask not, cries the holm-oak,
Weep, says snow.

STEVIE SMITH, "By a Holm-Oak"

Down goes the river
Down to the south
I've lost my ring
I've lost my soul
Go, sailor, go, but don't inquire
where I have hidden my own heart!
My heart is there there there
in no man's land.
Down go the winds
down go the clouds
I've lost my ring
I've lost my soul
Down goes the river
Down to the south
I'll never see again my ring, my ring,
I've for ever lost my soul, my soul.

Spiritual

There there now There there
O all those tears, yes, You feel so bad
O O O
All those tears
You just cry it out. We'll just sit here and rock
While you cry it out.

That's it. That's it.
There there there. Let's put this sweater round you.
   There there
You just have a good cry. Yes it's
Going to be alright. We'll just
Sit here and rock till you feel better.
You just cry it out till it's better.

JUDITH DUERK, from *Circle of Stones:*
A Woman's Journey to Herself

Time does not bring relief; you all have lied
   Who told me time would ease me of my pain!
   I miss him in the weeping of the rain;
I want him at the shrinking of the tide;
The old snows melt from every mountain-side,
   And last year's leaves are smoke in every lane;
   But last year's bitter loving must remain
Heaped on my heart, and my old thoughts abide!

There are a hundred places where I fear
   To go, — so with his memory they brim!
And entering with relief some quiet place
Where never fell his foot or shone his face
I say, "There is no memory of him here!"
   And so stand stricken, so remembering him!

EDNA ST. VINCENT MILLAY,
"Time does not bring relief"

There will be those to say in this mother-worshipping
culture that I am harsh, embittered. They will be quite

wrong. Why should I be embittered? It is far too late. A month ago, after a passage of many years, I stood above [my mother's] grave in a place called Wyuka. We, she and I, were close to being one now, lying like the skeletons of last year's leaves in a fence corner. And it was all nothing. Nothing, do you understand? All the pain, all the anguish. Nothing. We were, both of us, merely the debris life always leaves in its passing, like the maimed discarded chicks in a hatchery tray—no more than that. For a little longer I would see and hear, but it was nothing, and to the world it would mean nothing.

LOREN EISELEY, from *All the Strange Hours*

O dark dark dark. They all go into the dark,
The vacant interstellar spaces, the vacant into the
 vacant
. . .
I said to my soul, be still, and wait without hope,
For hope would be hope for the wrong thing; wait
 without love
For love would be love of the wrong thing; there is yet
 faith
But the faith and the love and the hope are all in the
 waiting.
Wait without thought, for you are not ready for
 thought

T. S. ELIOT, from "East Coker"

Are you still alone
in your cave of doubt   I
can't bear to think of you

there in that darkness   though
perhaps you have to be there

for a while to find your own
kind of light   did I help to

drive you there   though we
are far apart I try to reach

into your cave to hold your
hand   can you feel my touch

I hope you can know for a
moment that you're not alone.

JAMES LAUGHLIN, "Are You Still Alone"

Taurean reaper of the wild apple field
messenger from earthmire gleaning
transcripts of fog
in the nineteenth year and the eleventh month
speak your tattered Kaddish for all suicides:

Praise to life though it crumbled in like a tunnel
on ones we knew and loved

   Praise to life though its windows blew shut
   on the breathing-room of ones we knew and loved

Praise to life though ones we knew and loved
loved it badly, too well, and not enough

Praise to life though it tightened like a knot
on the hearts of ones we thought we knew loved us

Praise to life giving room and reason
to ones we knew and loved who felt unpraisable

Praise to them, how they loved it, when they could.
ADRIENNE RICH, "Tattered Kaddish"

God, I know nothing, my sense is all nonsense,
And fear of You begins intelligence:
Does it end there? For sexual love, for food,
For books and birch trees I claim gratitude,
But when I grieve over the unripe dead
My grief festers, corrupted into dread,
And I know nothing. Give us our daily bread.
DONALD HALL, "A Grace"

Do not go gentle into that good night,
Old age should burn and rave at close of day;
Rage, rage against the dying of the light.

Though wise men at their end know dark is right,
Because their words had forked no lightning they
Do not go gentle into that good night.

Good men, the last wave by, crying how bright
Their frail deeds might have danced in a green bay,
Rage, rage against the dying of the light.

Wild men who caught and sang the sun in flight,
And learn, too late, they grieved it on its way,
Do not go gentle into that good night.

Grave men, near death, who see with blinding sight
Blind eyes could blaze like meteors and be gay,
Rage, rage against the dying of the light.

And you, my father, there on the sad height,
Curse, bless, me now with your fierce tears, I pray.
Do not go gentle into that good night,
Rage, rage against the dying of the light.

DYLAN THOMAS,
"Do not go gentle into that good night"

In a dark time, the eye begins to see,
I meet my shadow in the deepening shade;
I hear my echo in the echoing wood—
A lord of nature weeping to a tree.
I live between the heron and the wren,
Beasts of the hill and serpents of the den.

What's madness but nobility of soul
At odds with circumstance? The day's on fire!
I know the purity of pure despair,
My shadow pinned against a sweating wall.

That place among the rocks—is it a cave,
Or winding path? The edge is what I have.

A steady storm of correspondences!
A night flowing with birds, a ragged moon,
And in broad day the midnight come again!
A man goes far to find out what he is—
Death of the self in a long, tearless night,
All natural shapes blazing unnatural light.

Dark, dark my light, and darker my desire.
My soul, like some heat-maddened summer fly,
Keeps buzzing at the sill. Which I is *I?*
A fallen man, I climb out of my fear.
The mind enters itself, and God the mind,
And one is One, free in the tearing wind.

THEODORE ROETHKE, "In a Dark Time"

The sky came carousing down around him. He saw the
sun drenching the green westward islands and batter-
ing a path down the water. He saw the town before him
to the south, where the trestle lighted down. Then far
on the Nooksack plain to the east, he saw a man walking. The distant figure was turning pea rows under in
perfect silence. He was dressed in horse's harness and
he pulled the plow. His feet trod his figure's long blue
shadow, and the plow cut its long blue shadow in the
ground. The man turned back as if to look along the
furrow, to check its straightness. Clare saw again, on
the plain farther north, another man; this one walked

behind a horse and turned the green ground under. Then before him on the trestle over the water he saw the earth itself walking, the earth walking darkly as it always walks in every season: it was plowing the men under, and the horses, and the plows.

ANNIE DILLARD, from *The Living*

Labyrinths
born of time
vanish.

(Only desert
remains.)

The heart,
fountain of desires,
vanishes.

(Only desert
remains.)

The illusion of dawn
and kisses
vanishes.

Only desert
remains.
Undulating
desert.

FEDERICO GARCÍA LORCA,
"And Then," translation by Norman Thomas Di Giovanni

Mysteries: What Is Death? What Are Time, Space, Transformation?

Myth, art, ritual; song, dance, prayer; religious doctrine and philosophical system: all these, together with science, which has become our modern mode of exploration of the Mysteries, may have been generated from a fundamental question in human experience: What of the dead? This question, spoken or unspoken, underlies the formulations of the funeral and memorial service.

Life is a dream, and a dream of a dream . . .
(La vida es sueño y sueño de sueño . . .)

CALDERÓN

The fear of death is the pretence of wisdom, and not real wisdom, being a pretence of knowing the unknown; and no one knows whether death, which men in their fear apprehend to be the greatest evil, may not be the greatest good. Is not this ignorance of a disgraceful sort, the ignorance which is the conceit that man knows what he does not know? . . .

[T]here is great reason to hope that death is a good; for one of two things—either death is a state of nothingness and utter unconsciousness, or, as men say, there is a change and migration of the soul from this world to another. Now if you suppose that there is no consciousness, but a sleep like the sleep of him who is undisturbed even by dreams, death will be an unspeakable gain. . . . Now if death be of such a nature, I say that to die is gain; for eternity is then only a single night. But if death is the journey to another place, and there, as men say, all the dead abide, what good, O my friends and judges, can be greater than this? . . . What would not a man give if he might converse with Orpheus and . . . Hesiod and Homer? Nay, if this be true, let me die again and again. . . . I shall then be able to continue my search into true and false knowledge; as in this world, so also in the next and I shall find out who is wise, and who pretends to be wise, and is not. What would not a man give, O judges, to be able to examine the leader of the great Trojan expedition; or Odysseus or Sisyphus, or numberless others, men and women too! What infinite delight would there be in conversing with them and asking them questions! In another world they do not put a man to death for asking ques-

tions: assuredly not. For besides being happier than we
are, they will be immortal, if what is said is true.

Wherefore, O judges, be of good cheer about death,
and know of a certainty, that no evil can happen to a
good man, either in life or after death.

PLATO, from *The Apology of Socrates*,
translation by B. Jowett

It must be so. Plato, thou reasonest well!
Else whence this pleasing hope, this fond desire,
This longing after immortality?
Or whence this secret dread, and inward horror
    of falling into naught? Why shrinks the soul
Back on herself, and startles at destruction?
'Tis the divinity that stirs within us.
'Tis Heaven itself that points out an hereafter
And intimates eternity to man.

. . .

The stars shall fade away, the sun himself
Grow dim with age, and Nature sink in years,
But thou shall flourish in immortal youth,
Unhurt amid the war of elements,
The wreck of matter, and the crush of worlds.

CATO, from "Soliloquy on Immortality,"
translation by Joseph Addison

[W]hen the body has perished there is an end also of
the spirit diffused through it. It is surely crazy to cou-
ple a mortal object with an eternal and suppose that
they can work in harmony and mutually interact. What

can be imagined more incongruous, what more repugnant and discordant, than that a mortal object and one that is immortal and everlasting should unite to form a compound and jointly weather the storms that rage about them? . . .

Equally vain is the suggestion that the spirit is immortal because it is shielded by life-preserving powers; or because it is unassailed by forces hostile to its survival; or because such forces, if they threaten, are somehow arrested before we are conscious of the threat. Apart from the spirit's participation in the ailments of the body, it has maladies of its own. The prospect of the future torments it with fear and wearies it with worry, and past misdeeds leave the sting of remorse. Lastly, it may fall a prey to the mind's own specific afflictions, madness and amnesia, and plunge into the black waters of oblivion.

From all this it follows that *death is nothing to us* and no concern of ours, since our tenure of the mind is mortal. In days of old, we felt no disquiet when the hosts of Carthage poured in to battle on every side—when the whole earth, dizzied by the convulsive shock of war, reeled sickeningly under the high ethereal vault, and between realm and realm the empire of mankind by land and sea trembled in the balance. So, when we shall be no more—when the union of body and spirit that engenders us has been disrupted—to us, who shall then be nothing, nothing by any hazard will happen any more at all.

LUCRETIUS, from *On the Nature of the Universe*, Book III,

translation by Ronald Latham

To be born, is to begin to be
Some other thing we were not formerly:
And what we call to die, is not t'appear,
Or be the thing that formerly we were.
Those very elements, which we partake
Alive, when dead some other bodies make:
Translated grow, have sense, or can discourse:
But death on deathless substance has no force.

. . .

All changing species should my song recite;
Before I ceas'd would change the day to night.
Nations and empires flourish and decay,
By turns command, and in their turn obey.

. . .

Thus Troy for ten long years her foes withstood,
And daily bleeding bore th' expence of blood;
Now for thick streets it shows an empty space.
Or only fill'd with tombs of her own perish'd race,
Herself becomes a sepulchre of what she was.

OVID, from *Metamorphoses*, Vol. 4, Book XV,
translation by John Dryden

Never say about anything, "I have lost it," but only
"I have given it back." Is your child dead? "It has
been given back." Is your wife dead? "She has been
given back." "I have had my farm taken away." Very
well, this too has been given back. "Yet it was a
rascal who took it away." But what concern is it of
yours by whose instrumentality the Giver called for its

return? So long as He gives it you, take care of it as of a thing that is not your own, as travellers treat their inn.

EPICTETUS, from *The Manual*,
translation by W. A. Oldfather

The six cardinal points, reaching into infinity, are ever included in Tao. An autumn spikelet, in all its minuteness, must carry Tao within itself. There is nothing on earth which does not rise and fall, but it never perishes altogether. The *Yin* and the *Yang*, and the four seasons, keep to their proper order. Apparently destroyed, yet really existing; the material gone, the immaterial left—such is the law of creation, which passeth all understanding. This is called the root, whence a glimpse may be obtained of God.

CHUANG TZU, from "The Mysterious Tao,"
in *Musings of a Chinese Mystic*

Upwards and downwards, from age to age, the cycles of the universe follow their unchanging round. It may be that the World-Mind wills each separate happening in succession; and if so, then accept the consequences. Or, it may be, there was but one primal act of will, of which all else is the sequel; every event being thus the germ of another. To put it another way, things are either isolated units, or they form one inseparable whole. If that whole be God, then all is well; but if aimless chance, at least you need not be aimless also.

Soon earth will cover us all. Then in time earth, too, will change; later, what issues from this change will itself in turn incessantly change, and so again will all that then takes its place, even unto the world's end. To let the mind dwell on these swiftly rolling billows of change and transformation is to know a contempt for all things mortal. . . . Look down from above on the numberless herds of mankind, with their mysterious ceremonies, their divers voyagings in storm and calm, and all the chequered pattern of their comings and gatherings and goings. Go on to consider the life of by-gone generations; and then the life of all those who are yet to come; . . . A little while, and all that is before your eyes now will have perished. . . . Loss is nothing else but change, and change is Nature's delight. . . . Even at this late hour, set yourself to become a simpler and better [person] in the sight of the gods. For that lesson, three years are as good as a hundred.

MARCUS AURELIUS, from *Meditations*,
translation by Maxwell Staniforth

Cowards die many times before their death;
The valiant never taste of death but once.
Of all the wonders that I yet have heard,
It seems to me most strange that men should fear;
Seeing that death, a necessary end,
Will come when it will come.

WILLIAM SHAKESPEARE, from *Julius Caesar*

When I consider the short duration of my life, my little space engulfed by the eternity before and after—that infinite immensity of space of which I am ignorant and which knows me not—I am fearful.

The eternal silence of those infinite spaces fills me with fear.

BLAISE PASCAL, from the *Pensées*

Human existence is girt round with mystery: the narrow region of our experience is a small island in the midst of a boundless sea. To add to the mystery, the domain of our earthly existence is not only an island of infinite space, but also in infinite time. The past and the future are alike shrouded from us: we neither know the origin of anything which is, nor its final destination.

JOHN STUART MILL

The only possible proof of the existence of water, the most convincing and the most intimately true proof, is thirst.

GASTON BACHELARD, quoting E. Susini

[T]ell him that we shall all bear his memory in the most precious part of our hearts, and that the world shall bow their heads to it, as our loves do. Tell him that the most sceptical of us has faith enough in the high things that nature puts into our heads, to think that all who are of one accord in mind and heart, are journeying to one and the same place, and shall unite somehow or other again face to face, mutually conscious, mutually delighted. Tell him he is only before us on the road, as he was in everything else, and that we are coming after him.

LEIGH HUNT, from a letter on the death of John Keats

> Be not curious about God,
> For I who am curious about each am not curious
>   about God,
> No array of terms can say how much I am at peace
>   about God and about death.

WALT WHITMAN

[I]n quitting this strange world, he now has gone a little ahead of me. This is of little significance. For us believing physicists, the separation of past, present, and future has only the character of an illusion.

ALBERT EINSTEIN, from a letter
on the death of physicist M. Besso

Some religions do not regard our sojourn on earth as true life. They either teach that everything appearing to us here is mere appearance, behind which we should penetrate, or that it is only a forecourt of the true world, a forecourt which we should cross without paying much attention to it. Judaism, on the contrary, teaches that what a man does now and here with holy intent is no less important, no less true—being a terrestrial indeed, but none the less factual, link with divine being—than the life in the world to come. This doctrine has found its fullest expression in Hasidism.

Rabbi Hanokh said: "The other nations too believe that there are two worlds. They too say: 'In the other world.' The difference is this: They think that the two are separate and severed, but Israel professes that the two worlds are essentially one and shall in fact become one."

In their true essence, the two worlds are one. They only have, as it were, moved apart. But they shall again become one, as they are in their true essence. Man was created for the purpose of unifying the two worlds. He contributes towards this unity by holy living, in relationship to the world in which he has been set, at the place on which he stands. . . .

MARTIN BUBER, from "Here Where One Stands,"
in *The Way of Man*

It is very hard to live with silence. The real silence is death . . . To approach this Silence, it is necessary to journey into the desert. You do not go into the desert to find identity but to lose it, to lose your personality, to become anonymous. You make yourself voiceless. You *become* silence. And then something extraordinary happens: you hear silence speak.

EDMOND JABES, from *The Book of Margins*

Are you still here? Are you standing in some
    corner?

  .   .   .

    If you are still here with me, if in this darkness
there is still some place where your spirit resonates
on the shallow soundwaves stirred up by my voice:
hear me; help me. We can so easily
slip back from what we have struggled to attain,
abruptly, into a life we never wanted;
can find that we are trapped, as in a dream,
and die there, without ever waking up.
This can occur.

  .   .   .

For somewhere there is an ancient enmity
between our daily life and the great work.
Help me, in saying it, to understand it.
    Do not return. If you can bear to, stay
dead with the dead. The dead have their own tasks.
But help me, if you can without distraction,
as what is farthest sometimes helps: in me.

RAINER MARIA RILKE, from "Requiem,"

translation by Stephen Mitchell

American Indian Poems

In the great night my heart will go out,
Toward me the darkness comes rattling,
In the great night my heart will go out.

from the Papago

Perchance do we truly live on earth?
Not forever on earth,
But briefly here!
Be it jade, it too will be broken;
Be it gold, it too will be melted,
And even the plume of the quetzal decays.
Not forever on earth,
But briefly here!

from the Aztec

The moon and the year
travel and pass away:
also the day, also the wind.
Also the flesh passes away
to the place of its quietness.

from the Maya

Death speaks: There was a merchant in Bagdad who sent his servant to market to buy provisions and in a little while the servant came back, white and trembling, and said, Master, just now when I was in the market-place I was jostled by a woman in the crowd and when I turned I saw it was Death that jostled me. She looked at me and made a threatening gesture; now, lend me your horse, and I will ride away from this city and avoid my fate. I will go to Samarra and there Death will not find me. The merchant lent him his horse, and the servant mounted it, and he dug his spurs in its flanks and as fast as the horse could gallop he went. Then the merchant went down to the market-place and he saw me standing in the crowd and he came to me and said, Why did you make a threatening gesture to my servant when you saw him this morning? That was not a threatening gesture, I said, it was only a start of surprise. I was astonished to see him in Bagdad, for I had an appointment with him tonight in Samarra.

W. SOMERSET MAUGHAM

Henry James

Isn't the highest deepest note of the whole thing the never-to-be-lost memory of that evening hour at Mount Auburn—at the Cambridge Cemetery when I took my way alone—after much waiting for the favouring hour—to that unspeakable group of graves. It was late, in November; the trees all bare, the dusk to fall early, the air all still (at Cambridge, in general, *so* still), with the western sky more and more turning to that terrible, deadly, pure polar pink that shows behind American winter woods. But I can't go over this—I can only, oh, so gently, so tenderly, brush it and breathe upon it— breathe upon it and brush it. It was the moment; it was the hour; it was the blessed flood of emotion that broke out at the touch of one's sudden *vision* and carried me away. I seemed then to know why I had done this; I seemed then to know why I had *come*—and to feel how not to have come would have been miserably, horribly to miss it. It made everything right—it made everything priceless. The moon was there, early, white and young, and seemed reflected in the white face of the great empty Stadium, forming one of the boundaries of Soldiers' Field, that looked over at me, stared over at me, through the clear twilight, from across the Charles. Everything was there, everything *came*; the recognition, stillness, the strangeness, the pity and the sanctity and the terror, the breath-catching passion and the divine relief of tears. William's inspired transcript, on the exquisite little Florentine urn of Alice's ashes, William's divine gift to us, and to her, of the Dantean lines—

Dopo lungo esilio e martiro
Viene a questa pace —

took me so at the throat by its penetrating *rightness*, that it was as if one sank down on one's knees in a kind of anguish of gratitude before something for which one had waited with a long, deep *ache*. But why do I write of the all unutterable and the all abysmal? Why does my pen not drop from my hand on approaching the infinite pity and tragedy of all the past? It does, poor helpless pen, with what it meets of the ineffable, what it meets of the cold Medusa-face of life, of all the life *lived*, on every side, *Basta, basta!*

from the *Notebook*

We living are a meager handful whose pathways briefly intersect in a flash of time, before we join the larger population of The Dead. Are we not but the rim, the outer edge, transiently illumined, of the world's people, the little passing as against the great passed?

from "The Altar of the Dead"

We die with the dying:
See, they depart, and we go with them.
We are born with the dead:
See, they return, and bring us with them.

T. S. ELIOT, from "Little Gidding"

It is a custom among the people, when throwing away water at night, to cry out in a loud voice, "Take care of the water"; or literally, from the Irish, "Away with yourself from the water"—for they say that the spirits of the dead last buried are then wandering about, and it would be dangerous if the water fell on them.

One dark night a woman suddenly threw out a pail of boiling water without thinking of the warning words. Instantly a cry was heard, as of a person in pain, but no one was seen. However, the next night a black lamb entered the house, having the back all fresh scalded, and it lay down moaning by the hearth and died. Then they all knew that this was the spirit that had been scalded by the woman, and they carried the dead lamb out reverently, and buried it deep in the earth. Yet every night at the same hour it walked again into the house, and lay down, moaned, and died; and after this had happened many times, the priest was sent for, and finally, by the strength of his exorcism, the spirit of the dead was laid to rest; the black lamb appeared no more. Neither was the body of the dead lamb found in the grave when they searched for it, though it had been laid by their own hands deep in the earth, and covered with clay.

LADY WILDE, "The Black Lamb,"

from *Irish Fairy and Folk Tales*,

edited by W. B. Yeats

Nature's first green is gold,
Her hardest hue to hold.
Her early leaf's a flower;
But only so an hour.

Then leaf subsides to leaf.
So Eden sank to grief,
So dawn goes down to day.
Nothing gold can stay.

ROBERT FROST, "Nothing Gold Can Stay"

Nothing that ever flew
Not the lark not you
Can die as others do.

AUTHOR UNKNOWN

How to resist nothingness? What power
Preserves what once was, if memory does not last?
For I remember little. I remember so very little

. . .

Do I believe in the Resurrection of the Flesh?
    Not of this ash.
I call, I beseech: elements, dissolve yourselves!
Rise into the other, let it come, kingdom!
Beyond the earthly fire compose yourselves anew!

CZESLAW MILOSZ, from "On Parting
with My Wife, Janina"

I have spent my life watching, not to see beyond the world, merely to see, great mystery, what is plainly before my eyes. I think the concept of transcendence is based on a misreading of creation. With all respect to heaven, the scene of the miracle is here, among us. The eternal as an idea is much less preposterous than time, and this very fact should seize our attention.

MARILYNNE ROBINSON, from *The Death of Adam*

Hope is a whirl of dead leaves, a reflection of their gold rustling in the wind.

EDMOND JABES, from *The Book of Margins*

It was beginning winter,
An in-between time,
The landscape still partly brown:
The bones of weeds kept swinging in the wind,
Above the blue snow.

It was beginning winter,
The light moved slowly over the frozen field,
Over the dry seed-crowns,
The beautiful surviving bones
Swinging in the wind.

Light traveled over the wide field;
Stayed.
The weeds stopped swinging.
The mind moved, not alone,
Through the clear air, in the silence.

Was it light?
Was it light within?
Was it light within light?
Stillness becoming alive,
Yet still?

A lively understandable spirit
Once entertained you.
It will come again.
Be still.
Wait.

THEODORE ROETHKE, from "The Lost Son"

Heroes and Heroines, Great and Simple

To write the names of the dead in stone
or memory, poetic language or the transformations of myth—this ancient intent
has found new expression in our time
in a kind of humane realism that cele-
brates the beloved plain and simple.
Voices of this latter kind will no doubt
be heard at a contemporary memorial
service, but they draw their dark reso-
nances from heroic funeral and memorial services of the past.

But I claim there will be some who remember us when we are gone.

SAPPHO, translation by Richmond Lattimore

[T]he wound Enkidu had received
In his struggle with Humbaba grew worse.
He tossed with fever and was filled with dreams.
He woke his friend to tell him what he heard and saw:
The gods have said that one of us must die
Because we killed Humbaba and the Bull of
   Heaven.

. . .

I know that they have chosen me.
The tears flowed from his eyes.
My brother, it is the fever only,
Said Gilgamesh.

. . .

Gilgamesh did not let himself believe
The gods had chosen one of them to die.

. . .

Gilgamesh knew his friend was close to death.
He tried to recollect aloud their life together
That had been so brief, so empty of gestures
They never felt they had to make. Tears filled his eyes
As he appealed to Ninsun, his mother, and to the
   Elders
Not to explain but to save his friend
Who once had run among the animals,
The wild horses of the range, the panther of the
   Steppe.
He had run and drunk with them
As if they were his brothers.
Just now he went with me into the forest of Humbaba
And killed the Bull of Heaven.

Everything had life to me, he heard Enkidu murmur,
The sky, the storm, the earth, water, wandering,
The moon and its three children, salt, even my hand
Had life. It's gone. It's gone. I have seen death

. . .

He looked at Gilgamesh, and said:
You will be left alone, unable to understand
In a world where nothing lives anymore
As you thought it did.

. . .

   [A] man sees death in things.
That is what it is to be a man. You'll know
When you have lost the strength to see
The way you once did. You'll be alone and wander
Looking for that life that's gone or some
Eternal life you have to find.
He drew closer to his friend's face.
My pain is that my eyes and ears
No longer see and hear the same
As yours do. Your eyes have changed.
You are crying. You never cried before.
It's not like you.
Why am I to die,
You to wander on alone?
Is that the way it is with friends?

Gilgamesh sat hushed as his friend's eyes stilled.
In his silence he reached out
To touch the friend whom he had lost.

from "The Death of Enkidu" in *Gilgamesh: A Verse Narrative*,
translation by Herbert Mason

The Almighty, aroused,
Called on the gods

. . .

   asked them to witness
That heaven and earth could be saved only
By what he now must do.

. . .

With a splitting crack of thunder he lifted a bolt,
Poised it by his ear,
Then drove the barbed flash point-blank into
   Phaethon.
The explosion
Snuffed the ball of flame
As it blew the chariot to fragments. Phaethon
Went spinning out of his life.

The crazed horses scattered.
They tore free, with scraps of the yoke,
Trailing their broken reins.
The wreckage fell through space,
Shattered wheels gyrating far apart,
Shards of the car, the stripped axle,
Bits of harness—all in slow motion
Sprinkled through emptiness.

Phaethon, hair ablaze,
A fiery speck, lengthening a vapour trail,
Plunged towards the earth
Like a star
Falling and burning out on a clear night.

In a remote land
Far from his home
The hot current
Of the broad Eridanus
Quenched his ember—
And washed him ashore.
The Italian nymphs
Buried his remains, that were glowing again
And flickering little flames
Of the three-forked fire from God.
Over his grave, on a rock they wrote this:
Here lies Phoebus' boy who died
In the sun's chariot.
His strength too human, and too hot
His courage and his pride.

OVID,

from "The Death of Phaethon,"

translation by Ted Hughes

This is the dust of Timas, who died before she was
married
and whom Persephone's dark chamber accepted
instead.
After her death the maidens who were her friends,
with sharp iron
cutting their lovely hair, laid it upon her tomb.

SAPPHO, "Epitaph,"

translation by Richmond Lattimore

Crito made a sign to the servant, who was standing by; and he went out, and having been absent for some time, returned with the jailer carrying the cup of poison. Socrates said: You, my good friend, who are experienced in these matters, shall give me directions how I am to proceed. The man answered: You have only to walk about until your legs are heavy, and then to lie down, and the poison will act. At the same time he handed the cup to Socrates, who in the easiest and gentlest manner, without the least fear or change of colour or feature, looking at the man with all his eyes, Echecrates, as his manner was, took the cup and said: What do you say about making a libation out of this cup to any god? May I, or not? The man answered: We only prepare, Socrates, just so much as we deem enough. I understand, he said: but I may and must ask the gods to prosper my journey from this to the other world—even so—and so be it according to my prayer. Then raising the cup to his lips, quite readily and cheerfully he drank off the poison. And hitherto most of us had been able to control our sorrow; but now when we saw him drinking, and saw too that he had finished the draught, we could no longer forbear, and in spite of myself my own tears were flowing fast; so that I covered my face and wept, not for him, but at the thought of my own calamity in having to part from such a friend.

Nor was I the first; for Crito, when he found himself unable to restrain his tears, had got up, and I followed; and at that moment, Apollodorus, who had been weeping all the time, broke out in a loud and passionate cry which made cowards of us all. Socrates alone retained his calmness: What is this strange outcry? he said. I sent away the women mainly in order that they might not misbehave in this way, for I have been told that a man should die in peace. Be quiet then, and have patience. When we heard his words we were ashamed, and refrained our tears; and he walked about until, as he said, his legs began to fail, and then he lay on his back, according to directions, and the man who gave him the poison now and then looked at his feet and legs; and after a while he pressed his foot hard, and asked him if he could feel; and he said, No; and then his leg, and so upwards and upwards, and showed us that he was cold and stiff. And he felt them himself, and said: When the poison reaches the heart, that will be the end. He was beginning to grow cold about the groin, when he uncovered his face, for he had covered himself up, and said—they were his last words—he said: Crito, I owe a cock to Asclepius; will you remember to pay the debt? The debt shall be paid, said Crito; is there anything else? There was no answer to this question; but in a minute or two a movement was heard, and the attendants uncovered him; his eyes were set, and Crito closed his eyes and mouth.

Such was the end, Echecrates, of our friend; concerning whom I may truly say, that of all men of his time whom I have known, he was the wisest and justest and best.

PLATO, from *The Phaedo*,
translation by B. Jowett

When they saw Patroklos dead
—so brave and strong, so young—
the horses of Achilles began to weep;
their immortal nature was upset deeply
by this work of death they had to look at.
They reared their heads, tossed their long manes,
beat the ground with their hooves, and mourned
Patroklos, seeing him lifeless, destroyed,
now mere flesh only, his spirit gone,
defenseless, without breath,
turned back from life to the great Nothingness.

C. P. CAVAFY, from "The Horses of Achilles,"
translation by Edmund Keeley and Philip Sherrard

During the same winter [of 431–430 B.C.E.], in ac-
cordance with an old national custom, the funeral of
those who first fell in this war was celebrated by the
Athenians. The ceremony is as follows: Three days before the celebration they erect a tent in which the bones
of the dead are laid out, and every one brings to his
own dead any offering which he pleases. At the time of
the funeral the bones are placed in chests of cypress
wood, which are conveyed on hearses; there is one
chest for each tribe. They also carry a single empty litter decked with a pall for all whose bodies are missing,
and cannot be recovered after the battle. . . . The public
sepulchre is situated in the most beautiful spot outside
the walls; there they always bury those who fall in war;
only after the battle of Marathon the dead, in recognition of their pre-eminent valor, were interred on the
field. When the remains have been laid in the earth,

some man of known ability and high reputation, chosen by the city, delivers a suitable oration over them; after which the people depart. Such is the manner of interment; and the ceremony was repeated from time to time throughout the war. Over those who were the first buried Pericles was chosen to speak. At the fitting moment he advanced from the sepulchre to a lofty stage, which had been erected in order that he might be heard as far as possible by the multitude, and spoke as follows:

"I will speak first of our ancestors, for it is right and becoming that now, when we are lamenting the dead, a tribute should be paid to their memory. There has never been a time when they did not inhabit this land, which by their valor they have handed down from generation to generation, and we have received from them a free state. But if they were worthy of praise, still more were our fathers, who added to their inheritance, and after many a struggle transmitted to us their sons this great empire. . . .

"Our form of government does not enter into rivalry with the institutions of others. We do not copy our neighbors, but are an example to them. It is true that we are called a democracy, for the administration is in the hands of the many and not of the few. But while the law secures equal justice to all alike in their private disputes, the claim of excellence is also recognized; and when a citizen is in any way distinguished, he is preferred to the public service, not as a matter of privilege, but as the reward of merit. Neither is poverty a bar, but a man may benefit his country whatever be the obscurity of his condition. There is no exclusiveness in our public life, and in our private intercourse we are not suspicious of one another, nor angry with our neighbor if he does what he likes; . . .

"We are lovers of the beautiful, yet simple in our tastes, and we cultivate the mind without loss of manliness. Wealth we employ, not for talk and ostentation, but when there is a real use for it. To avow poverty with us is no disgrace: the true disgrace is in doing nothing to avoid it. An Athenian citizen does not neglect the state because he takes care of his own household; and even those of us who are engaged in business have a very fair idea of politics. . . . To sum up: I say that Athens is the school of Hellas, and that the individual Athenian in his own person seems to have the power of adapting himself to the most varied forms of action with the utmost versatility and grace. . . . [T]here are mighty monuments of our power which will make us the wonder of this and of succeeding ages; we shall not need the praises of Homer or of any other panegyrist. . . . For we have compelled every land and every sea to open a path for our valor, and have everywhere planted eternal memorials of our friendship and of our enmity. Such is the city for whose sake these men nobly fought and died; . . . on the battle-field their feet stood fast, and in an instant, at the height of their fortune, they passed away from the scene, not of their fear, but of their glory.

"Such was the end of these men; they were worthy of Athens. . . . the whole earth is the sepulchre of famous men; not only are they commemorated by columns and inscriptions in their own country, but in foreign lands there dwells also an unwritten memorial of them, graven not on stone but in the hearts of men."

THUCYDIDES,
from *History of the Peloponnesian War*

[W]e do rate you first of men,
both in the common crises of our lives
and face-to-face encounters with the gods.

SOPHOCLES, from *Oedipus the King*

Dido, we have not the means to repay your goodness,
  nor have
Any of our kin, wherever they are, scattered over the
  world.
If angels there be who look after the good, if indeed
  just dealing
And minds informed with the right mean anything to
  heaven,
May God reward you as you deserve! What happy age,
What great parentage was it gave life to the like of
  you?
So long as rivers run to the sea, and shadows wheel
  round
The hollows of the hills, and star-flocks browse in the
  sky,
Your name, your fame, your glory shall perish not
  from the land.

VIRGIL, from *The Aeneid*,
translation by Cecil Day Lewis

[T]he warriors rode around the barrow,
twelve of them in all, athelings' sons.
They recited a dirge to declare their grief,
spoke of the man, mourned their King.
They praised his manhood and the prowess of his
  hands,
they raised his name; it is right a man
should be lavish in honouring his lord and friend,
should love him in his heart when the leading-forth
from the house of flesh befalls him at last.

This was the manner of the mourning of the men of
  the Geats,
sharers in the feast, the fall of their lord:
they said that he was of all the world's kings
the gentlest of men, and the most gracious,
the kindest to his people, the keenest for fame.

from *Beowulf*, translation by Michael Alexander

Tell me now in what hidden way is
  Lady Flora the lovely Roman?
Where's Hipparchia, and where is Thaïs,
  Neither of them the fairer woman?
  Where is Echo, beheld of no man,
Only heard on river and mere, —
  She whose beauty was more than human? . . .
But where are the snows of yester-year?

Where's Héloise, the learned nun,
  For whose sake Abeillard, I ween,
Lost manhood and put priesthood on?

(From Love he won such dule and teen!)
   And where, I pray you, is the Queen
Who willed that Buridan should steer
   Sewed in a sack's mouth down the Seine? . . .
But where are the snows of yester-year?

White Queen Blanche, like a queen of lilies,
   With a voice like any mermaiden, —
Bertha Broadfoot, Beatrice, Alice,
   And Ermengarde the lady of Maine, —
   And that good Joan whom Englishmen
At Rouen doomed and burned her there, —
   Mother of God, where are they then? . . .
But where are the snows of yester-year?

Nay, never ask this week, fair lord,
   Where they are gone, nor yet this year,
Save with this much for an overword, —
   But where are the snows of yester-year?

               FRANÇOIS VILLON, "The Ballad of Dead Ladies,"
                       translation by Dante Gabriel Rossetti

[N]ow I see the true old times are dead,
When every morning brought a noble chance,
And every chance brought out a noble knight.
Such times have been not since the light that led
The holy Elders with the gift of myrrh.
But now the whole Round Table is dissolved
Which was an image of the mighty world,
And I, the last, go forth companionless,

And the days darken round me, and the years,
Among new men, strange faces, other minds.

    And slowly answer'd Arthur from the barge:
'The old order changeth, yielding place to new,
And God fulfils himself in many ways.
. . .
If thou shouldst never see my face again,
Pray for my soul. More things are wrought by prayer
Than this world dreams of. Wherefore, let thy voice
Rise like a fountain for me night and day.
For what are men better than sheep or goats
That nourish a blind life within the brain,
If, knowing God, they lift not hands of prayer
Both for themselves and those who call them friend?
For so the whole round earth is every way
Bound by gold chains about the feet of God.
But now farewell. I am going a long way
With these thou seest—if indeed I go
(For all my mind is clouded with a doubt)—
To the island-valley of Avilion;
Where falls not hail, or rain, or any snow,
Nor ever wind blows loudly; but it lies
Deep-meadow'd, happy, fair with orchard lawns
And bowery hollows crown'd with summer sea,
Where I will heal me of my grievous wound.'

    So said he, and the barge with oar and sail
Moved from the brink, like some full-breasted swan
That, fluting a wild carol ere her death,
Ruffles her pure cold plume, and takes the flood

With swarthy webs. Long stood Sir Bedivere
Revolving many memories, till the hull
Look'd one black dot against the verge of dawn,
And on the mere the wailing died away.

   But when that moan had past for evermore,
The stillness of the dead world's winter dawn
Amazed him, and he groaned, 'The King is gone.'
And therewithal came on him the weird rhyme,
'From the great deep to the great deep he goes.'

   Whereat he slowly turn'd and slowly clomb
The last hard footstep of that iron crag;
Thence mark'd the black hull moving yet, and cried,
'He passes to be King among the dead,
And after healing of his grievous wound
He comes again.'
.   .   .
   Thereat once more he moved about, and clomb
Even to the highest he could climb, and saw,
Straining his eyes beneath an arch of hand,
Or thought he saw, the speck that bare the King,
Down that long water opening on the deep
Somewhere far off, pass on and on, and go
From less to less and vanish into light.
And the new sun rose bringing the new year.

                    ALFRED, LORD TENNYSON,
                         from *Idylls of the King*

Shakespeare

The ripest fruit falls first . . .

from Richard II

CAESAR: I am constant as the northern star,
Of whose true-fixt and resting quality
There is no fellow in the firmament.
The skies are painted with unnumber'd
    sparks,
They are all fire, and every one doth shine;
But there's but one in all doth hold his
    place:
So in the world,—'tis furnisht well with
    men,
And men are flesh and blood, and
    apprehensive;
Yet in the number I do know but one
That unassailable holds on his rank,
Unshaked of motion: and that I am he.

from Julius Caesar

MARCUS ANTONIUS: His life was gentle; and the
    elements
So mixt in him, that Nature
    might stand up
And say to all the world,
    "This was a man!"

from Julius Caesar

HORATIO: Now cracks a noble heart.—good night,
                 sweet prince;
             And flights of angels sing thee to thy rest!

from Hamlet

❦

He was not of an age, but for all time;
And all the Muses still were in their prime,
When, like Apollo, he came forth to warm
Our ears, or like a Mercury to charm.
Nature herself was proud of his designs,
And joy'd to wear the dressing of his lines;
Which were so richly spun, and woven so fit,
As since she will vouchsafe no other wit:
The merry Greek, tart Aristophanes,
Neat Terence, witty Plautus, now not please;
But antiquated and deserted lie,
As they were not of Nature's family.
Yet must I not give Nature all; thy art,
My gentle Shakespeare, must enjoy a part:
For though the poet's matter nature be,
His art doth give the fashion; and that he
Who casts to write a living line, must sweat,—
Such as thine are,—and strike the second heat
Upon the Muses' anvil; turn the same,
And himself with it, that he thinks to frame;
Or, for the laurel, he may gain a scorn,—
For a good poet's made, as well as born

And such wert thou.

. . .

I see thee in the hemisphere
Advanced, and made a constellation there:
Shine forth, thou star of poets, and with rage
Or influence chide or cheer the drooping stage;
Which, since thy flight from hence, hath mourn'd like
  night,
And despairs day, but for thy volume's light.

BEN JONSON, from "To the memory of my beloved,
the author, Master William Shakespeare,
and what he hath left us"

My dearest dust, could not thy hasty day
Afford thy drowzy patience leave to stay
One hower longer: so that we might either
Sate up, or gone to bedd together?
But since thy finisht labor hath possest
Thy weary limbs with early rest,
Enjoy it sweetly: and thy widdowe bride
Shall soone repose her by thy slumbering side.
Whose business, now, is only to prepare
My nightly dress, and call to prayre:
Mine eyes wax heavy and ye day growes old.
The dew falls thick, my beloved growes cold.
Draw, draw ye closed curtaynes: and make room:
My dear, my dearest dust; I come, I come.

LADY CATHERINE DYER, "My Dearest Dust"
*(Epitaph on monument erected in 1641 by
Lady Catherine Dyer to her husband Sir William Dyer
in Colmworth Church, Bedfordshire)*

He was my friend, the truest friend on earth;
A strong and mighty influence joined our birth.
Nor did we envy the most sounding name
    By friendship given of old to fame.
None but his brethren he, and sister, knew
Whom the kind youth preferred to me;
And even in that we did agree,
For much above myself I loved them too.

Say, for you saw us, ye immortal lights,
How oft unwearied have we spent the nights?
Till the Ledæan stars, so famed for love,
    Wondered at us from above,
We spent them not in toys, in lusts, or wine,
    But search of deep philosophy,
    Wit, eloquence, and poetry,
Arts which I loved, for they, my friend, were thine.

ABRAHAM COWLEY,
from "On the Death of Mr. William Hervey"

Here lies a gentleman bold
Who was so very brave
He went to lengths untold,
And on the brink of the grave
Death had on him no hold.
By the world he set small store —
He frightened it to the core —
Yet somehow, by Fate's plan,

Though he'd lived a crazy man,
When he died he was sane once more.

MIGUEL DE CERVANTES, from Don Quixote,
translation by Samuel Putnam

Remember me when I am gone away,
  Gone far away into the silent land;
  When you can no more hold me by the hand,
Nor I half turn to go yet turning stay.
Remember me when no more day by day
  You tell me of our future that you planned:
  Only remember me; you understand
It will be late to counsel then or pray.
Yet if you should forget me for a while
  And afterwards remember, do not grieve:
  For if the darkness and corruption leave
  A vestige of the thoughts that once I had,
Better by far you should forget and smile
  Than that you should remember and be sad.

CHRISTINA ROSSETTI, "Remember"

Not a drum was heard, not a funeral note
As his corpse to the ramparts we hurried.
Not a soldier discharged his farewell shot
O'er the grave where our hero we buried.

We buried him darkly at dead of night,
The sods with our bayonets turning.
By the struggling moonbeams' misty light
And the lantern dimly burning.

No useless coffin enclosed his breast,
Not in sheet nor in shroud we bound him,
But he lay like a warrior taking his rest
With his martial cloak around him.

CHARLES WOLFE,
from "The Burial of Sir John Moore at Coruña"

Under the wide and starry sky
Dig the grave and let me lie:
Glad did I live and gladly die,
   And I laid me down with a will.

This be the verse you grave for me:
Here he lies where he long'd to be;
Home is the sailor, home from the sea,
   And the hunter home from the hill.

ROBERT LOUIS STEVENSON, "Requiem"

❧

Mourn for Polly Botsford, aged thirty-nine,
and for her blossom Polly, one year old,
and for Gideon, her infant son, nipped in the bud.
And mourn for the mourners under the graveside
   willow,
trailing its branches of inverted V's,
those women propped like bookends on either side of
   the tomb,
and that brace of innocents in matching calico

linked to their mother's grief with a zigzag clasp of
    hands,
as proper in their place as stepping-stones.
Mourn, too, for the nameless painter of the scene
who, like them all, was born to walk a while
beside the brook whose source is common tears,
till suddenly it's time to unlatch the narrow gate
and pass through the church that is not made with
    walls
and seek another home, a different sky.

   Bless in a congregation, because they are so numer-
ous, those industrious schoolgirls stitching their alpha-
bets; and the deft ones with needles at lacework,
crewel, knitting; and mistresses of spinning, weaving,
dyeing; and daughters of tinsmiths painting their orna-
mental mottoes; and hoarders of rags hooking and
braiding their rugs; and adepts in cutouts, valentines,
stencils, still lifes, and "fancy pieces"; and middleaged
housewives painting, for the joy of it, landscapes and
portraits; and makers of bedcovers with names that
sing in the night—Rose of Sharon, Princess Feather, De-
lectable Mountains, Turkey Tracks, Drunkard's Path,
Indiana Puzzle, Broken Dishes, Star of LeMoyne, Cur-
rants and Coxcomb, Rocky-Road-to-Kansas.

   Bless them and greet them as they pass from their
long obscurity, through the gate that separates us from
our history, a moving rainbow-cloud of witnesses in a
rising hubbub, jubilantly turning to greet one another,
this tumult of sisters.

   STANLEY KUNITZ, from "A Blessing of Women"

Ralph Waldo Emerson

[A] true man belongs to no other time and place, but is the center of things. Where he is, there is nature. He measures you, and all men, and all events. You are constrained to accept his standard. . . . This all great men are and do. Every true man is a cause, a country, and an age; requires infinite spaces and numbers and time fully to accomplish his thought—and posterity seem to follow his steps as a procession . . . and millions of minds so grow and cleave to his genius that he is confounded with virtue and the possible [*sic*] of man. An institution is the lengthened shadow of one man . . . and all history resolves itself very easily into the biography of a few stout and earnest persons.

from "Self-Reliance"

Fall, stream, from Heaven to bless; return as well;
So did our sons; Heaven met them as they fell.

Inscription for a well in memory of the martyrs of the war

A march in the ranks hard-prest, and the road
  unknown,
A route through a heavy wood with muffled steps in
  the darkness,

Our army foil'd with loss severe, and the sullen
  remnant retreating,
Till after midnight glimmer upon us the lights of a
  dim-lighted building,
We come to an open space in the woods, and halt by
  the dim-lighted building,
'Tis a large old church at the crossing roads, now an
  impromptu hospital,
Entering but for a minute I see a sight beyond all the
  pictures and poems ever made,
Shadows of deepest, deepest black, just lit by moving
  candles and lamps,
And by one great pitchy torch stationary with wild red
  flame and clouds of smoke,
By these, crowds, groups of forms vaguely I see on the
  floor, some in the pews laid down,
At my feet more distinctly a soldier, a mere lad, in danger
  of bleeding to death, (he is shot in the abdomen,)
I stanch the blood temporarily, (the youngster's face is
  white as a lily,)
Then before I depart I sweep my eyes o'er the scene
  fain to absorb it all,
Faces, varieties, postures beyond description, most in
  obscurity, some of them dead,
Surgeons operating, attendants holding lights, the
  smell of ether, the odor of blood,
The crowd, O the crowd of the bloody forms, the yard
  outside also fill'd,
Some on the bare ground, some on planks or
  stretchers, some in the death-spasm sweating,
An occasional scream or cry, the doctor's shouted
  orders or calls,

The glisten of the little steel instruments catching the
    glint of the torches,
These I resume as I chant, I see again the forms, I
    smell the odor,
Then hear outside the orders given, *Fall in, my men, fall
    in;*
But first I bend to the dying lad, his eyes open, a half-
    smile gives he me,
Then the eyes close, calmly close, and I speed forth to
    the darkness,
Resuming, marching, ever in darkness marching, on in
    the ranks,
The unknown road still marching.

WALT WHITMAN, "A March in the Ranks
Hard-Prest, and the Road Unknown"

About noon, when Major Pendleton came into the
room, he asked, "Who is preaching at headquarters today?" He was told that Mr. Lacy was, and that the
whole army was praying for him. "Thank God," he
said; "they are very kind to me." Already his strength
was fast ebbing, and although his face brightened when
his baby was brought to him his mind had begun to
wander. Now he was on the battlefield, giving orders to
his men; now at home in Lexington; now at prayers in
the camp. Occasionally his senses came back to him,
and about half-past one he was told that he had but two
hours to live. Again he answered, feebly but firmly,
"Very good; it is all right." These were almost his last
coherent words. For some time he lay unconscious, and
then suddenly he cried out: "Order A. P. Hill to pre-

pare for action! Pass the infantry to the front! Tell Major Hawks . . ." then stopped, leaving the sentence unfinished. Once more he was silent; but a little while after he said very quietly and clearly, "Let us cross over the river, and rest under the shade of the trees," and the soul of the great captain passed into the peace of God.

LIEUTENANT COLONEL GEORGE
FRANCIS ROBERT HENDERSON,
"The Death of Stonewall Jackson"

Swift has sailed into his rest;
Savage indignation there
Cannot lacerate his breast.
Imitate him if you dare,
World-besotted traveller; he
Served human liberty.

W. B. YEATS, "Swift's Epitaph"

For a season there must be pain —
For a little, little space
I shall lose the sight of her face,
Take back the old life again
While She is at rest in her place.

For a season this pain must endure,
For a little, little while
I shall sigh more often than smile
Till Time shall work me a cure,
And the pitiful days beguile.

For that season we must be apart,
For a little length of years,
Till my life's last hour nears,
And, above the beat of my heart,
I hear Her voice in my ears.

But I shall not understand—
Being set on some later love,
Shall not know her for whom I strove,
Till she reach me forth her hand,
Saying, 'Who but I have the right?'
And out of a troubled night
Shall draw me safe to the land.

RUDYARD KIPLING, "The Widower"

Sorrow is my own yard
where the new grass
flames as it has flamed
often before but not
with the cold fire
that closes round me this year.
Thirtyfive years
I lived with my husband.
The plumtree is white today
with masses of flowers.
Masses of flowers
load the cherry branches
and color some bushes
yellow and some red
but the grief in my heart

is stronger than they
for though they were my joy
formerly, today I notice them
and turn away forgetting.
Today my son told me
that in the meadows,
at the edge of the heavy woods
in the distance, he saw
trees of white flowers.
I feel that I would like
to go there
and fall into those flowers
and sink into the marsh near them.

WILLIAM CARLOS WILLIAMS,
"The Widow's Lament in Springtime"

Lives of great men all remind us
    We can make our lives sublime,
And, departing, leave behind us
    Footprints on the sands of time.

HENRY WADSWORTH LONGFELLOW,
from "A Psalm of Life"

They told me, Heraclitus, they told me you were dead,
They brought me bitter news to hear and bitter tears
    to shed
I wept as I remembered how often you and I
Had tired the sun with talking and sent him down the
    sky.

And now that thou art lying, my dear old Carian guest
A handful of gray ashes, long, long ago at rest,
Still are thy pleasant voices, thy nightingales, awake;
For Death, he taketh all away, but them he cannot
    take.

WILLIAM JOHNSON-CORY, "Heraclitus"

Bergotte never went out of doors, and when he got out
of bed for an hour in his room, he would be smothered
in shawls, plaids, all the things with which a person
covers himself before exposing himself to intense cold
or getting into a railway train. He would apologise to
the few friends whom he allowed to penetrate to his
sanctuary, and, pointing to his tartan plaids, his travel-
ling-rugs, would say merrily: "After all, my dear fellow,
life, as Anaxagoras has said, is a journey." Thus he
went on growing steadily colder, a tiny planet that offered a prophetic image of the greater, when gradually
heat will withdraw from the earth, then life itself. Then
the resurrection will have to come to an end, for if,
among future generations, the works of men are to
shine, there must first of all be men. . . . [The] circumstances of his death were as follows. An attack of
uraemia, by no means serious, had led to his being or-
dered to rest. But one of the critics having written
somewhere that in *Vermeer's Street in Delft* (lent by the
Gallery at The Hague for an exhibition of Dutch painting), a picture which he adored and imagined that he
knew by heart, a little patch of yellow wall (which he

could not remember) was so well painted that it was, if one looked at it by itself, like some priceless specimen of Chinese art, of a beauty that was sufficient in itself, Bergotte ate a few potatoes, left the house, and went to the exhibition. At the first few steps that he had to climb he was overcome by giddiness. He passed in front of several pictures and was struck by the stiffness and futility of so artificial a school, nothing of which equalled the fresh air and sunshine of a Venetian palazzo, or of an ordinary house by the sea. At last he came to the Vermeer which he remembered as more striking, more different from anything else that he knew, but in which, thanks to the critic's article, he re-marked for the first time some small figures in blue, that the ground was pink, and finally the precious sub-stance of the tiny patch of yellow wall. His giddiness increased; he fixed his eyes, like a child upon a yellow butterfly which it is trying to catch, upon the precious little patch of wall. "That is how I ought to have writ-ten," he said. "My last books are too dry, I ought to have gone over them with several coats of paint, made my language exquisite in itself, like this little patch of yellow wall." Meanwhile he was not unconscious of the gravity of his condition. In a celestial balance there ap-peared to him, upon one of its scales, his own life, while the other contained the little patch of wall so beauti-fully painted in yellow. . . .

He repeated to himself: "Little patch of yellow wall, with a sloping roof, little patch of yellow wall." While doing so he sank down upon a circular divan; and then at once he ceased to think that his life was in jeopardy and, reverting to his natural optimism, told himself: "It is just an ordinary indigestion from those potatoes; they weren't properly cooked; it is nothing." A fresh attack beat him down; he rolled from the divan to the floor, as visitors and attendants came hurrying to his assistance. He was dead. Permanently dead? Who shall say? . . . All that we can say is that everything is arranged in this life as though we entered it carrying the burden of obligations contracted in a former life; there is no reason inherent in the conditions of life on this earth that can make us consider ourselves obliged to do good, to be fastidious, to be polite even, nor make the talented artist consider himself obliged to begin over again a score of times a piece of work the admiration aroused by which will matter little to his body devoured by worms, like the patch of yellow wall painted with so much knowledge and skill by an artist who must for ever remain unknown and is barely identified under the name Vermeer. All these obligations which have not their sanction in our present life seem to belong to a different world, founded upon kindness, scrupulosity, self-sacrifice, a world entirely different from this; which we leave in order to be born into this world, before perhaps returning to the other to live once again beneath the sway of those unknown laws which we have obeyed because we bore their precepts in our hearts, knowing not whose hand had traced them there . . .

They buried him, but all through the night of mourning, in the lighted windows, his books arranged three by three kept watch like angels with outspread wings and seemed, for him who was no more, the symbol of his resurrection.

MARCEL PROUST, from *The Past Recaptured*,
translation by Frederick A. Blossom

According to the admitted standards of greatness, Jefferson was a great man. After all deductions on which his enemies might choose to insist, his character could not be denied elevation, versatility, breadth, insight and delicacy . . . he fairly reveled in what he believed to be beautiful, and his writings often betrayed subtle feeling for artistic form, — a sure mark of intellectual sensuousness. He shrank from whatever was rough or coarse, and his yearning for sympathy was almost feminine.

HENRY ADAMS, from *History of the United States
of America During the First Administration of Thomas Jefferson*

Do not grieve for me too much. I am a spirit confident of my rights. Death is only an incident, & not the most important wh[ich] happens to us in this state of being. On the whole, especially since I met you my darling one I have been happy, & you have taught me how noble a woman's heart can be. If there is anywhere else I shall be on the look out for you. Meanwhile look forward, feel free, rejoice in Life, cherish the children, guard my memory. God bless you.

WINSTON CHURCHILL, from a letter to his wife,
"In the event of my death . . ."

In Flanders fields the poppies blow
Between the crosses, row on row
That mark our place: and in the sky
The larks still bravely singing, fly
Scarce heard amid the guns below.

We are the Dead. Short days ago
We lived, felt dawn, saw sunset glow,
Loved, and were loved, and now we lie
In Flanders fields.

Take up our quarrel with the foe:
To you from failing hands we throw
The Torch: be yours to hold it high!
If ye break faith with us who die
We shall not sleep, though poppies grow
In Flanders fields.

JOHN McCRAE,
"In Flanders Fields"

He stirs, beginning to awake.
A kind of ache
Of knowing troubles his blind warmth; he moans,
And the high hammering drone
Of the first crossing fighters shakes
His sleep to pieces, rakes
The darkness with its skidding bursts, is done.
All that he has known

Floods in upon him; but he dreads
The crooked thread
Of fire upon the darkness: "The great drake
Flutters to the icy lake—
The shotguns stammer in my head.

I lie in my own bed,"
He whispers, "dreaming"; and he thinks to wake.
The old mistake.

A cot creaks; and he hears the groan
He thinks his own—
And groans, and turns his stitched, blind, bandaged
   head
Up to the tent-flap, red
With dawn. A voice says, "Yes, this one";
His arm stings; then, alone,
He neither knows, remembers—but instead
Sleeps, comforted.

. . .

The tags' chain stirs with the wind; and I sleep
Paid, dead, and a soldier. Who fights for his own life
Loses, loses: I have killed for my world, and am free.
                    RANDALL JARRELL, "A Field Hospital"

The friends of my father
Stand like gnarled trees
Yet in their eyes I see
Spring's crinkled leaf

And thus, although one dies
With nothing to bequeath
We are left enough
Love to make us grieve

SAMUEL MENASHE,
"The friends of my father"

Sundays too my father got up early
and put his clothes on in the blueblack cold,
then with cracked hands that ached
from labor in the weekday weather made
banked fires blaze. No one ever thanked him.

I'd wake and hear the cold splintering, breaking.
When the rooms were warm, he'd call,
and slowly I would rise and dress,
fearing the chronic angers of that house,

Speaking indifferently to him,
who had driven out the cold
and polished my good shoes as well.
What did I know, what did I know
of love's austere and lonely offices?

ROBERT HAYDEN, "Those Winter Sundays"

Buffalo Bill 's
defunct
        who used to
        ride a watersmooth-silver
                        stallion
and break onetwothreefourfive pigeonsjustlikethat
                                Jesus
he was a handsome man
                    and what i want to know is
how do you like your blueeyed boy
Mr. Death

E. E. CUMMINGS, "Buffalo Bill 's"

Grandad's gone
who used to
shoot grouse
and deliver onetwothreefourfive babies
just like that
    By Jiminy
He was a tough and tender man
and what I want to know is
How did you stop those big healing hands
Mister Death

CLYDE WATSON, "Portrait
(modelled after ee cummings)"

you came to me
and woke me in the night
small disheveled figure tumbled out
with dragging sheets

hurrying to
quit the sight of monsters and the
inquisitive snout of that
intrusive stranger
death

you crept into my bed
and shivering curled against me
your firm blossoming cheek
beneath my hand
I felt your round knees
digging comfort from my
warm belly

the fiends and shapes then
leaped
from your narrow
wishbone breast
you after all had
cried sanctuary
and landed fully operative
into my dreams

and in my dreams
there was nothing ranged
father nor mother nor
god
to annul that
dark decree

NANCY DINGMAN WATSON, "you came to me"

I think of that grave woman in the dark
There by the delicate stream at the pitch of moon,
Valor encompassed by the rare serene.
Difficult life has battered her and yet
With what magnificent strength she outstands that
No matter that the earth be dark and worn.
Might I learn, wasted and much torn,
From whence she gets the laughter of her kind.
Giving and blessing, it enkindles mind
And on the heart its wisdom without rancor fiery-
    earned
Bestows such light that all seems round
And brought to full, like our redemptive moon.

JEAN GARRIGUE, "For J."

In times when nothing stood
but worsened, or grew strange,
there was one constant good:
            she did not change.

PHILIP LARKIN, "In times when nothing stood"

Timeless Praise in
Scripture and Verse

To let the sensibility find such acute expression that in each node or pulse of verbal sound, *meaning* is compacted to release its implications only over time: this was the power of voices speaking out of the sky in ancient times, still heard in the ears of certain poets and writers today.

Loveliest of what I leave behind is the sunlight,
and loveliest after that the shining stars, and the
moon's face,
but also cucumbers that are ripe, and pears, and
apples.
PRAXÍLLA OF SÍCYON, translation by Richmond Lattimore

I live, I die, I am Osiris.
I have entered you, and have reappeared through you.
I have waxed fat in you.
I have grown in you.
I have fallen upon my side.
The gods are living from me.

.   .   .

I live, I die, I am barley.

from "Prayer for Osiris,"
rendered by Otto Eberhard

God said, This is the token of the covenant which I make between me and you and every living creature that is with you, for perpetual generations: I do set my bow in the cloud, and it shall be for a token of a covenant between me and the earth. And it shall come to pass, when I bring a cloud over the earth, that the bow shall be seen in the cloud: And I will remember my covenant, which is between me and you and every living creature of all flesh; and the waters shall no more become a flood to destroy all flesh. And the bow shall be in the cloud; and I will look upon it, that I may remember the everlasting covenant between God and every living creature of all flesh that is upon the earth. And God said unto Noah, This is the token of the covenant, which I have established between me and all flesh that is upon the earth.

Genesis 11:1–9 (King James Version)

For a small moment have I forsaken thee; but with great mercies will I gather thee.

In a little wrath I hid my face from thee for a moment, but with everlasting kindness will I have mercy on thee . . .

For the mountains shall depart, and the hills be removed; but my kindness shall not depart from thee, neither shall the covenant of my peace be removed . . .

O thou afflicted, tossed with tempest, and not comforted, behold, I will lay thy stones with fair colors, and lay thy foundations with sapphires.

And I will make thy windows of agates, and thy gates of carbuncles, and all thy borders of pleasant stones.

And great shall be the peace of thy children.

Isaiah 54:7–13 (King James Version)

The Lord giveth, the Lord taketh away, blessed be the name of the Lord. As we recall the beloved ones who have passed away, these words bring healing to the hurt that death has wrought. Our loved ones have answered the summons that sound for all men, for we are sojourners upon earth and our times are in His hands. We loose our hold upon life when our time is come, as the leaf falls from the bough when its day is done. The deeds of the righteous enrich the lives of men as the fallen leaf enriches the soil beneath. The dust returns to the earth, the spirit lives on with God's eternal years. Like the stars by day, our beloved dead are not seen with mortal eyes, but they shine on in the untroubled

firmament of endless time. Let us be thankful for the
companionship that continues in love that is stronger
than death and spans the gulf of the grave. Cherishing
their memory, let us, in the presence of the congregation, sanctify the name of God.

from a funeral service in
The Union Prayerbook

Magnified and sanctified
may His great name be
in the world that He created,
as He wills,
and may His kingdom come
in your lives and in your days,
and in the lives of all the house of Israel,
swiftly and soon,
and say all amen!

Amen!
May His great Name be blessed
always and forever!

Blessed
and praised
and glorified
and raised
and exalted
and honored
and uplifted
and lauded
be the Name of the Holy One

(He is blessed!)
above all blessings
and hymns and praises and consolations
that are uttered in the world,
and say all amen!

May a great peace from heaven—
and life!—
be upon us and upon all Israel,
and say all amen!

May He who makes peace in His high places
make peace upon us and upon all Israel,
and say all amen!

The Kaddish

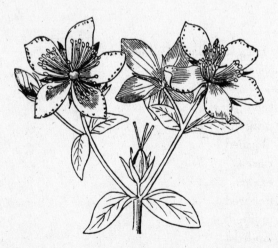

Psalms (KING JAMES VERSION)

What is man, that thou art mindful of him? and the son of man, that thou visitest him?

For thou hast made him a little lower than the angels, and hast crowned him with glory and honour.

Thou madest him to have dominion over the works of thy hands; thou hast put all things under his feet:

All sheep and oxen, yea, and the beasts of the field;

The fowl of the air, and the fish of the sea, and whatsoever passeth through the paths of the seas.

O Lord our Lord, how excellent is thy name in all the earth!

from Psalm 8

Deep calleth unto deep at the noise of thy waterspouts: all thy waves and thy billows are gone over me.

Yet the Lord will command his lovingkindness in the daytime, and in the night his song shall be with me, and my prayer unto the God of my life.

I will say unto God my rock, Why hast thou forgotten me? why go I mourning because of the oppression of the enemy?

As with a sword in my bones, mine enemies reproach me; while they say daily unto me, Where is thy God?

Why art thou cast down, O my soul? and why art thou disquieted within me? hope thou in God: for I shall yet praise him, who is the health of my countenance, and my God.

from Psalm 42

Lord, thou hast been our dwelling place in all generations.

Before the mountains were brought forth, or ever thou hadst formed the earth and the world, even from everlasting to everlasting, thou art God.

Thou turnest man to destruction; and sayest, Return, ye children of men.

For a thousand years in thy sight are but as yesterday when it is past, and as a watch in the night.

Thou carriest them away as with a flood; they are as a sleep: in the morning they are like grass which groweth up.

In the morning it flourisheth, and groweth up; in the evening it is cut down, and withereth.

For we are consumed by thine anger, and by thy wrath are we troubled.

Thou hast set our iniquities before thee, our secret sins in the light of thy countenance.

For all our days are passed away in thy wrath: we spend our years as a tale that is told.

The days of our years are threescore years and ten; and if by reason of strength they be fourscore years, yet is their strength labour and sorrow; for it is soon cut off, and we fly away.

Who knoweth the power of thine anger? even according to thy fear, so is thy wrath.

So teach us to number our days, that we may apply our hearts unto wisdom.

from Psalm 90

I will lift up mine eyes unto the hills, from whence cometh my help.

My help cometh from the Lord, which made heaven and earth.

He will not suffer thy foot to be moved: he that keepeth thee will not slumber.

Behold, he that keepeth Israel shall neither slumber nor sleep.

The Lord is thy keeper: the Lord is thy shade upon thy right hand.

The sun shall not smite thee by day, nor the moon by night.

The Lord shall preserve thee from all evil: he shall preserve thy soul.

The Lord shall preserve thy going out and thy coming in from this time forth, and even for evermore.

Psalm 121

For everything there is a season, and a time for every matter under heaven:

a time to be born, and a time to die;
a time to plant, and a time to pluck up what is
    planted;
a time to kill, and a time to heal;
a time to break down, and a time to build up;
a time to weep, and a time to laugh;
a time to mourn, and a time to dance;

a time to cast away stones, and a time to gather
    stones together;
a time to embrace, and a time to refrain from
    embracing;
a time to seek, and a time to lose;
a time to keep, and a time to cast away;
a time to rend, and a time to sew;
a time to keep silence, and a time to speak;
a time to love . . .

                        Ecclesiastes 3:1–8 (King James Version)

Blessed are they that mourn, for they shall be comforted.

                              Matthew 5:4 (King James Version)

Eternal Light, You only dwell within
Yourself, and only You know You; Self-knowing,
Self-known, You love and smile upon Yourself!
    That circle—which, begotten so, appeared
in You as light reflected—when my eyes
had watched it with attention for some time,
    within itself and colored like itself,
to me seemed painted with our effigy,

so that my sight was set on it completely.
    As the geometer intently seeks
to square the circle, but he cannot reach,
through thought on thought, the principle he needs,
    so I searched that strange sight: I wished to see
the way in which our human effigy
suited the circle and found place in it —
    and my own wings were far too weak for that.
But then my mind was struck by light that flashed
and, with this light, received what it had asked.
    Here force failed my high fantasy; but my
desire and will were moved already — like
a wheel revolving uniformly — by
    the Love that moves the sun and the other stars.

DANTE, from *The Divine Comedy: The Paradiso*,
translation by Allen Mandelbaum

O Great Spirit . . . Here at the center of the world,
where you took me when I was young and taught me
. . . I recall the great vision you sent me. It may be that
some little root of the sacred tree still lives. Nourish it,
then, that it may leaf and bloom and fill with singing
birds . . . Hear me for my people. Hear me that they
may once more go back into the sacred hoop and find
the good red road, the shielding tree!

BLACK ELK, from *Black Elk Speaks*

Glory be to God for dappled things —
    For skies of couple-colour as a brinded cow;
        For rose-moles all in stipple upon trout that swim;

Fresh-firecoal chestnut-falls; finches' wings;
　　Landscape plotted and pieced—fold, fallow, and
　　　　　　　　　　　　　　　　　　plough;
　　　And all trades, their gear and tackle and trim.

All things counter, original, spare, strange;
　　Whatever is fickle, freckled (who knows how?)
　　　With swift, slow; sweet, sour; adazzle, dim;
He fathers-forth whose beauty is past change:
　　　　Praise him.
　　　　　　　　GERARD MANLEY HOPKINS, "Pied Beauty"

　They that love beyond the World, cannot be
　　separated by it.
　Death cannot kill, what never dies.
　Nor can Spirits ever be divided that love and live in
　　the same
Divine Principle; the Root and Record of their
　Friendship.
　If Absence be not death, neither is theirs.

　Death is but Crossing the World, as Friends do the
　　Seas; they live in one another still.
　　　　　　　WILLIAM PENN, from "Union of Friends"

Amazing grace! How sweet the sound
That saved a wretch like me.
I once was lost and now am found,
Was blind but now I see.

'Twas grace that taught my heart to fear
And grace my fears relieved.
How precious did that grace appear
The hour I first believed.

Through many dangers, toils and snares
I have already come.
'Tis grace that brought me safe this far
And grace will lead me home.

from "Amazing Grace"

I know not where His islands lift
   Their fronded palms in air;
I only know I cannot drift
   Beyond His love and care.

JOHN GREENLEAF WHITTIER,
from "The Eternal Goodness"

Lead, kindly Light! amid the encircling gloom;
   Lead thou me on!
The night is dark, and I am far from home;
   Lead thou me on!
Keep thou my feet: I do not ask to see
The distant scene; one step enough for me.

So long thy power hath blessed me, sure it still
   Will lead me on,
O'er moor and fen, o'er crag and torrent, till
   The night is gone;

And with the morn, those angel faces smile
Which I have loved long since, and lost a while.

JOHN HENRY NEWMAN,
from "The Pillar of the Cloud"

A thousand ages in Thy sight
   Are like an evening gone;
Short as the watch that ends the night
   Before the rising sun.

Time, like an ever-rolling stream,
   Bears all its sons away;
They fly forgotten, as a dream
   Dies at the opening day.

O God, our help in ages past;
   Our hope for years to come;
Be Thou our guard while troubles last,
   And our eternal home!

ISAAC WATTS,
from "O God, Our Help"

There is no suffering for the one who has finished the journey and left sorrow behind, who has let go of all bonds to the world. Such human beings take their leave with their thoughts in order. They do not seek a new home. Like swans who have left their lake, they abandon house and home.

Buddhist aphorism, from *The Dhammapada*,
translation by Irving Babbitt

The Valley and the Spirit never die.
They form what is called the Mystic Mother,
from whose gate come heaven and earth.
She seems ever to endure,
Never to be emptied.

Heaven is long-lasting and the earth long-enduring,
for they do not live for themselves.
In the same way, the wise man forgets himself and is
    preserved.

The world is a divine vessel;
It cannot be shaped,
Nor can it be enforced.
Who shapes it, damages it;
who forces himself on it loses it.

Take care with the end as you do with the beginning.

LAO-TZU, from the Tao Te Ching

Before heaven and earth were, Tao was. It has existed
without change from all time. Spiritual beings drew
their spirituality therefrom, while the universe became
what we can see it now. To Tao, the zenith is not high,
nor the nadir low; no point in time is long ago, nor by
lapse of ages has it grown old. . . .

   The universe is very beautiful, yet it says nothing.
The four seasons abide by a fixed law, yet they are not
heard. All creation is based upon absolute principles,
yet nothing speaks.

   And the true Sage, taking his stand upon the beauty

of the universe, pierces the principles of created things. Hence the saying that the perfect man does nothing, the true Sage performs nothing, beyond gazing at the universe.

For man's intellect, however keen, face to face with the countless evolutions of things, their death and birth, their squareness and roundness,—can never reach the root. There creation is, and there it has ever been.

CHUANG TZU, from *Musings of a Chinese Mystic*,
translation by H. A. Giles

To Janaka, king of Videha, came once Yājñavalkya, who . . . promised to grant the king any wish and the king chose to ask questions. Therefore Janaka, king of Videha, began and asked this question:

Yājñavalkya, what is the light of man?

The sun is his light, O king, he answered. It is by the light of the sun that a man rests, goes forth, does his work and returns.

This is so in truth, Yājñavalkya. And when the sun is set, what is then the light of man?

The moon then becomes his light, he replied. It is by the light of the moon that a man rests, goes forth, does his work and returns.

This is so in truth, Yājñavalkya. And when the sun and the moon are set, what is then the light of man?

Fire then becomes his light. It is by the light of fire that a man rests, goes forth, does his work and returns.

And when the sun and the moon are set, Yājñavalkya, and the fire has sunk down, what is then the light of man?

Voice then becomes his light; and by voice as his light he rests, goes forth, does his work and returns. Therefore in truth, O king, when a man cannot see even his own hand, if he hears a voice after that he wends his way.

This is so in truth, Yājñavalkya. And when the sun is set, Yājñavalkya, and the moon is also set, and the fire has sunk down, and the voice is silent, what is then the light of man?

The Soul then becomes his light; and by the light of the Soul he rests, goes forth, does his work and returns.

What is the Soul? asked then the king of Videha.

Yājñavalkya spoke:

It is the consciousness of life. It is the light of the heart. . . . The Spirit of man wanders in the world of waking life and also in the world of dreams. He seems to wander in thought. He seems to wander in joy.

But in the rest of deep sleep he goes beyond this world and beyond its fleeting forms. When the Spirit of man . . . takes a body, then he is joined with mortal evils; but when at death he goes beyond, then he leaves evil behind.

The Spirit of man has two dwellings: this world and the world beyond. There is also a third dwelling-place: the land of sleep and dreams. Resting in this borderland the Spirit of man can behold his dwelling in this world and in the other world. Wandering in this borderland he beholds behind him the sorrows of this

world and in front of him he sees the joys of the beyond.

Hindu teachings, from *The Upanishads*,
translation by J. Mascaro

Be Thou praised, my Lord, with all Thy creatures,
   above all Brother Sun,
   who gives the day and lightens us therewith.

.   .   .

Be Thou praised, my Lord, of Sister Moon and the
      stars,
   in the heaven hast Thou formed them, clear and
      precious and comely.

Be Thou praised, my Lord, of Brother Wind,
   and of the air, and the cloud, and of fair and of all
      weather,

.   .   .

Be Thou praised, my Lord, of Sister Water,
   which is much useful and humble and precious and
      pure,

Be Thou praised, my Lord, of Brother Fire,
   by which Thou hast lightened the night,
   and he is beautiful and joyful and robust and strong.

Be Thou praised, my Lord, of our Sister Mother
      Earth,
   which sustains and hath us in rule,
   and produces divers fruits with coloured flowers
      and herbs.

Be Thou praised, my Lord, of those who pardon for
    Thy love
  and endure sickness and tribulations.

Blessed are they who will endure it in peace,
  for by Thee, Most High, they shall be crowned.

Be Thou praised, my Lord, of our Sister Bodily Death,
  from whom no man living may escape.
  Woe to those who die in mortal sin:

Blessed are they who are found in Thy most holy will,
  for the second death shall not work them ill.

Praise ye and bless my Lord, and give Him thanks,
  and serve Him with great humility.

SAINT FRANCIS OF ASSISI,
from *The Mirror of Perfection*

George Herbert

Sweet day, so cool, so calm, so bright,
The bridal of the earth and sky;
The dew shall weep thy fall to-night,
       For thou must die.

Sweet rose, whose hue angry and brave
Bids the rash gazer wipe his eye;
Thy root is ever in its grave,
       And thou must die.

Sweet spring, full of sweet days and roses,
A box where sweets compacted lie;
My musick shows ye have your closes,
       And all must die.

Only a sweet and virtuous soul,
Like season'd timber, never gives;
But though the whole world turn to coal,
       Then chiefly lives.

                           "Virtue"

    My God, I heard this day,
That none doth build a stately habitation,
   But he that means to dwell therein.
   What house more stately hath there been,
Or can be, than is man? to whose creation
    All things are in decay,

For Man is ev'ry thing,
And more: He is a tree, yet bears more fruit;
    A beast, yet is, or should be more:
    Reason and speech we only bring.
Parrots may thank us, if they are not mute,
        They go upon the score.

        Man is all symmetry,
Full of proportions, one limb to another,
    And all to all the world besides:
    Each part may call the furthest brother:
For head with foot hath private amity,
        And both with moons and tides.

        Nothing hath got so far,
But man hath caught and kept it, as his prey.
    His eyes dismount the highest star;
    He is in little all the sphere;
Herbs gladly cure our flesh; because that they
        Find their acquaintance there.

        For us the winds do blow,
The earth doth rest, heav'n move, and fountains flow,
    Nothing we see, but means our good,
    As our delight, or as our treasure:
The whole is either our cupboard of food
        Or cabinet of pleasure.

        The stars have us to bed;
Night draws the curtain, which the sun withdraws;
    Music and light attend our head.
    All things unto our flesh are kind

In their descent and being; to our mind
   In their ascent and cause

. . .

      Since then, my God, thou hast
So brave a palace built; O dwell in it,
   That it may dwell with thee at last!
   Till then, afford us so much wit;
That, as the world serves us, we may serve thee,
      And both thy servants be.

from "Man"

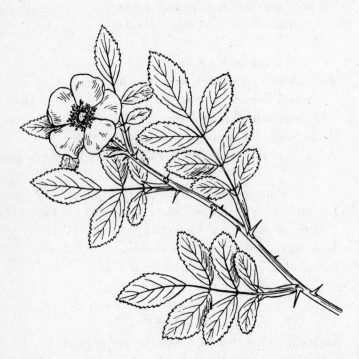

Henry Vaughan

They are all gone into the world of light!
   And I alone sit ling'ring here;
Their very memory is fair and bright,
   And my sad thoughts doth clear.

It glows and glitters in my cloudy brest
   Like stars upon some gloomy grove,
Or those faint beams in which this hill is drest,
   After the sun's remove.

I see them walking in an air of glory,
   Whose light doth trample on my days:
My days, which are at best but dull and hoary,
   Mere glimmering and decays.

. . .

Dear, beauteous Death! the Jewel of the Just,
   Shining no where, but in the dark;
What mysteries do lie beyond thy dust;
   Could man outlook that mark!

. . .

O Father of eternal life, and all
   Created glories under Thee!
Resume Thy spirit from this world of thrall
   Into true liberty.

Either disperse these mists, which blot and fill
   My perspective still as they pass,
Or else remove me hence unto that hill,
   Where I shall need no glass.

from "Friends Departed"

There is in God (some say)
A deep, but dazling darkness; As men here
Say it is late and dusky, because they
        See not all clear
    O for that night! where I in him
    Might live invisible and dim.

from "The Night"

Death, be not proud, though some have calléd thee
Mighty and dreadful, for thou art not so;
For those whom thou think'st thou dost overthrow
Die not, poor Death, nor yet canst thou kill me.
From rest and sleep, which but thy pictures be,
Much pleasure; then from thee much more must flow,
And soonest our best men with thee do go,
Rest of their bones, and soul's delivery.
Thou art slave to fate, chance, kings, and desperate
    men,
And dost with poison, war, and sickness dwell,
And poppy or charms can make us sleep as well,
And better than thy stroke; why swell'st thou then?
One short sleep past, we wake eternally
And death shall be no more; Death, thou shalt die.

JOHN DONNE, "Death, be not proud"

He is made one with Nature: there is heard
His voice in all her music, from the moan

Of thunder, to the song of night's sweet bird;
He is a presence to be felt and known
In darkness and in light, from herb and stone,
Spreading itself where'er that Power may move
Which has withdrawn his being to its own;
Which wields the world with never-wearied love,
Sustains it from beneath, and kindles it above.

He is a portion of the loveliness
Which once he made more lovely: he doth bear
His part, while the one Spirit's plastic stress
Sweeps through the dull dense world, compelling
    there,
All new successions to the forms they wear;
Torturing th' unwilling dross that checks its flight
To its own likeness, as each mass may bear;
And bursting in its beauty and its might
From trees and beasts and men into the Heaven's
    light.

The splendours of the firmament of time
May be eclipsed, but are extinguished not;
Like stars to their appointed height they climb,
And death is a low mist which cannot blot
The brightness it may veil. When lofty thought
Lifts a young heart above its mortal lair,
And love and life contend in it, for what
Shall be its earthly doom, the dead live there
And move like winds of light on dark and stormy air.

The One remains, the many change and pass;
Heaven's light forever shines, Earth's shadows fly;

Life, like a dome of many-coloured glass,
Stains the white radiance of Eternity.

.   .   .

Whilst, burning through the inmost veil of
    Heaven,
The soul of Adonais, like a star,
Beacons from the abode where the Eternal are.

PERCY BYSSHE SHELLEY,

from "Adonais: An Elegy on the

Death of John Keats"

Our birth is but a sleep and a forgetting:
The soul that rises with us, our life's star,
        Hath had elsewhere its setting,
            And cometh from afar;
        Not in entire forgetfulness,
        And not in utter nakedness,
But trailing clouds of glory do we come
        From God, who is our home:

.   .   .

    Though nothing can bring back the hour
Of splendour in the grass, of glory in the flower;
        We will grieve not, rather find
        Strength in what remains behind;
        In the primal sympathy
        Which having been must ever be;
        In the soothing thoughts that spring
        Out of human suffering;
        In the faith that looks through death,
In years that bring the philosophic mind.

.   .   .

Thanks to the human heart by which we live,
Thanks to its tenderness, its joys, and fears,
To me the meanest flower that blows can give
Thoughts that do often lie too deep for tears.

WILLIAM WORDSWORTH,
from "Ode:
Intimations of Immortality from
Recollections of Early Childhood"

Once out of nature I shall never take
My bodily form from any natural thing,
But such a form as Grecian goldsmiths make
Of hammered gold and gold enamelling
To keep a drowsy Emperor awake;
Or set upon a golden bough to sing
To lords and ladies of Byzantium
Of what is past, or passing, or to come.

W. B. YEATS,
from "Sailing to Byzantium"

What thou lovest well remains, the rest is dross
What thou lov'st well shall not be reft from thee
What thou lov'st well is thy true heritage

The ant's a centaur in his dragon world.
Pull down thy vanity, it is not man
Made courage, or made order, or made grace,

Pull down thy vanity, I say pull down.

EZRA POUND, from "Canto CXIV"

When earth's last picture is painted, and the tubes are
    twisted and dried,
When the oldest colors have faded, and the youngest
    critic has died,
We shall rest, and faith, we shall need it—lie down for
    an aeon or two,
Till the Master of All good Workmen shall set us to
    work anew!

And those that were good shall be happy; they shall sit
    in a Golden chair;
They shall splash at a ten-league canvas with brushes
    of comet's hair;
They shall find real saints to draw from—Magdalene,
    Peter and Paul;
They shall work for an age at a sitting and never be
    tired at all;

And only the Master shall praise us and only the
    Master shall blame;
And no one shall work for money, and no one shall
    work for fame
But each for the joy of the working and each in his
    separate star,
Shall draw the Thing as he sees It, for the God of
    Things as They Are.

                    RUDYARD KIPLING, "L'envoi"

Abide with me; fast falls the eventide;
The darkness deepens; Lord, with me abide;

When other helpers fail, and comforts flee,
Help of the helpless, O abide with me.

Swift to its close ebbs out life's little day;
Earth's joys grow dim, its glories pass away;
Change and decay in all around I see;
O Thou, who changest not, abide with me.

I need Thy presence every passing hour;
What but Thy grace can foil the tempter's power?
Who like Thyself my guide and stay can be?
Through cloud and sunshine, O abide with me.

HENRY FRANCIS LYTE, "Eventide"

Center of all centers, core of cores,
almond self-enclosed and growing sweet—
all this universe, to the furthest stars
and beyond them, is your flesh, your fruit.

Now you feel how nothing clings to you;
your vast shell reaches into endless space,
and there the rich, thick fluids rise and flow.
Illuminated in your infinite peace,

a billion stars go spinning through the night,
blazing high above your head.
But *in* you is the presence that
will be, when all the stars are dead.

RAINER MARIA RILKE, "Buddha in Glory,"
translation by Stephen Mitchell

Meditations on Wisdom
Coming Slowly

It comes not quickly nor easily, but in-
evitably in time: one's acceptance of
this ultimate rupture in our personal
and collective life as the natural out-
come of our origin in nature.

What's the meaning of all song?
"Let all things pass away."

W. B. YEATS, from "Vacillation"

Gentle lady, do not sing
   Sad songs about the end of love;
Lay aside sadness and sing
   How love that passes is enough.

JAMES JOYCE

Thou hast come safe to port,
I am still at sea
The light is on thy head,
Darkness in me.
Pluck thou in Heaven's field,
violet and rose
While I strew flowers
That will thy vigil keep
Where thou dost sleep,
Love, in thy last repose.

Ninth-century lyric written for the
Abbess of Grandestine, who died young

KNOWLEDGE: Everyman, I will go with thee and be thy
   guide.
   In thy most need to go by thy side.
EVERYMAN [*kneeling*]: I come with Knowledge for my
   redemption,
   Redempt with heart and full contrition . . .
KNOWLEDGE: Now hath he suffered that we all shall
   endure,
   The Good Deeds shall make all sure.
   Now hath he made ending.
   Methinketh that I hear angels sing.

And make great joy and melody
Where Everyman's soul received shall be.

from *Everyman*

So passeth, in the passing of a day,
   Of mortall life the leafe, the bud, the flowre;
   Ne more doth flourish after first decay,
   That earst was sought to decke both bed and bowre,
   Of many a ladie, and many a paramowre:
   Gather therefore the rose, whilest yet is prime,
   For soone comes age that will her pride deflowre:
   Gather the rose of love, whilest yet is time,
Whilest loving thou mayst lovèd be with equall crime.

EDMUND SPENSER, from *The Faerie Queen*

Now, now that the sun hath veil'd his light
And bid the world goodnight,
To the soft bed my body I dispose,
But where shall my soul repose?
Dear God, even in thy arms, and can there be
Any so sweet security?
Then to thy rest, O my soul, and, singing, praise
The mercy that prolongs thy days!
Alleluia.

WILLIAM FULLER, "Evening Hymn"

  Brave flowers, that I could gallant it like you
And be as little vain.

  .   .   .

Oh, teach me to see death and not to fear,
But rather to take truce;
How often have I seen you at a bier,
And there look fresh and spruce;
You fragrant flowers then teach me that my breath
Like yours may sweeten, and perfume my death.

HENRY KING, from "A Contemplation upon Flowers"

Heav'n from all creatures hides the book of Fate,
All but the page prescrib'd, their present state:
From brutes what men, from men what spirits know:
Or who could suffer Being here below?
The lamb thy riot dooms to bleed to-day,
Had he thy Reason, would he skip and play?
Pleas'd to the last, he crops the flow'ry food,
And licks the hand just rais'd to shed his blood.
Oh blindness to the future! kindly giv'n,
That each may fill the circle mark'd by Heav'n:
Who sees with equal eye, as God of all,
A hero perish, or a sparrow fall,
Atoms or systems into ruin hurl'd,
And now a bubble burst, and now a world.
    Hope humbly then; with trembling pinions soar;
Wait the great teacher Death, and God adore.
What future bliss, he gives not thee to know,
But gives that Hope to be thy blessing now.
Hope springs eternal in the human breast:
Man never Is, but always To be blest:
The soul, uneasy and confin'd from home,
Rests and expatiates in a life to come.

. . .

All are but parts of one stupendous whole,
Whose body Nature is, and God the soul;
That, chang'd thro' all, and yet in all the same;
Great in the earth, as in th' æthereal frame;
Warms in the sun, refreshes in the breeze,
Glows in the stars, and blossoms in the trees,
Lives thro' all life, extends thro' all extent,
Spreads undivided, operates unspent;
Breathes in our soul, informs our mortal part,
As full, as perfect, in a hair as heart.

. . .

All Nature is but Art, unknown to thee;
All Chance, Direction, which thou canst not see;
All Discord, Harmony not understood;
All partial Evil, universal Good:
And, spite of Pride, in erring Reason's spite,
One truth is clear, Whatever is, is right.

ALEXANDER POPE,
from *An Essay on Man*

Music, when soft voices die,
Vibrates in the memory;
Odors, when sweet violets sicken,
Live within the sense they quicken.

Rose leaves, when the rose is dead,
Are heaped for the belovèd's bed;
And so thy thoughts, when thou art gone,
Love itself shall slumber on.

PERCY BYSSHE SHELLEY, "To____"

Ah Love! could you and I with Him conspire
To grasp this sorry Scheme of Things entire.
Would not we shatter it to bits—and then
Remould it nearer to the Heart's Desire!

Yon rising Moon that looks for us again—
How oft hereafter will she wax and wane:
How oft hereafter rising look for us
Through this same Garden—and for one in vain!

And when like her, oh Saki, you shall pass
Among the guests star-scatter'd on the Grass.
And in your joyous errand reach the spot
Where I made One—turn down an empty Glass!

from *The Rubáiyát of Omar Khayyám*,
translation by Edward Fitzgerald

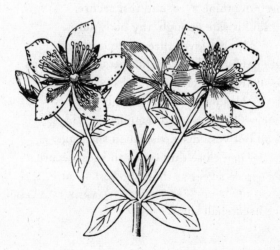

Sunset and evening star,
    And one clear call for me!
And may there be no moaning of the bar,
    When I put out to sea.

But such a tide as moving seems asleep,
    Too full for sound and foam,
When that which drew from out the boundless deep
    Turns again home.

Twilight and evening bell,
    And after that the dark!
And may there be no sadness of farewell,
    When I embark

ALFRED, LORD TENNYSON,
from "Crossing the Bar"

Close now thine eyes, and rest secure;
Thy soul is safe enough, thy body sure;
        He that loves thee, he that keeps
And guards thee, never slumbers, never sleeps.
The smiling conscience in a sleeping breast
        Has only peace, has only rest;
        The music and the mirth of kings,
Are all but very discords, when she sings;
        Then close thine eyes and rest secure;
No sleep so sweet as thine, no rest so sure.

FRANCIS QUARLES, "A Good-Night"

Shakespeare

Orpheus with his lute made trees,
And the mountain-tops that freeze,
    Bow themselves, when he did sing:
To his music plants and flowers
Ever sprung; as sun and showers
    There had made a lasting spring.

Every thing that heard him play,
Even the billows of the sea,
    Hung their heads, and then lay by.
In sweet music is such art,
Killing care and grief of heart
    Fall asleep, or hearing, die.

Song, from *Henry VIII*

Fear no more the heat o' the sun,
   Nor the furious winter's rages;
Thou thy worldly task hast done,
   Home art gone, and ta'en thy wages;
Golden lads and girls all must
   As chimney-sweepers, come to dust.

Fear no more the frown o' the great,
   Thou art past the tyrant's stroke:
Care no more to clothe and eat;
   To thee the reed is as the oak;
The sceptre, learning, physic, must
   All follow this, and come to dust.

Fear no more the lightning-flash,
    Nor the all-dreaded thunder-stone;
Fear not slander, censure rash;
    Thou hast finish'd joy and moan;
All lovers young, all lovers must
    Consign to thee, and come to dust.

No exorciser harm thee!
    Nor no witchcraft charm thee!
Ghost unlaid forbear thee!
    Nothing ill come near thee!
Quiet consummation have;
    And renownèd be thy grave!

"Dirge," from *Cymbeline*

PROSPERO: Our revels now are ended. These our
                actors,
             As I foretold you, were all spirits, and
             Are melted into air, into thin air:
             And, like the baseless fabric of this vision,
             The cloud-capp'd towers, the gorgeous
                palaces,
             The solemn temples, the great globe itself,
             Yea, all which it inherit, shall dissolve,
             And, like this insubstantial pageant faded,
             Leave not a rack behind. We are such
                stuff
             As dreams are made on; and our little life
             Is rounded with a sleep. —

from *The Tempest*

Once again

Do I behold these steep and lofty cliffs,
That on a wild, secluded scene impress
Thoughts of more deep seclusion; and connect
The landscape with the quiet of the sky.
The day is come when I again repose
Here, under this dark sycamore, and view
These plots of cottage-ground, these orchard-tufts.
Which at this season, with their unripe fruits,
Are clad in one green hue, and lose themselves
'Mid groves and copses. Once again I see
These hedge-rows, hardly hedge-rows, little lines
Of sportive wood run wild: these pastoral farms,
Green to the very door; and wreaths of smoke
Sent up, in silence from among the trees!
. . .

And I have felt

A presence that disturbs me with the joy
Of elevated thoughts; a sense sublime
Of something far more deeply interfused,
Whose dwelling is the light of setting suns,
And the round ocean and the living air,
And the blue sky, and in the mind of man;
A motion and a spirit, that impels
All thinking things, all objects of all thought,
And rolls through all things. Therefore am I still
A lover of the meadows and the woods,
And mountains; and of all that we behold

From this green earth; of all the mighty world
Of eye, and ear, — both what they half create,
And what perceive; well pleased to recognise
In nature and the language of the sense,
The anchor of my purest thoughts, the nurse,
The guide, the guardian of my heart, and soul
Of all my moral being.

WILLIAM WORDSWORTH,
from "Lines Composed a
Few Miles Above Tintern Abbey"

The poetry of earth is never dead:
　　When all the birds are faint with the hot sun,
　　And hide in cooling trees, a voice will run
From hedge to hedge about the new-mown mead:
That is the Grasshopper's — he takes the lead
　　In summer luxury, — he has never done
　　With his delights; for when tired out with fun
He rests at ease beneath some pleasant weed.
The poetry of earth is ceasing never:
　　On a lone winter evening, when the frost
　　　　Has wrought a silence, from the stove there
　　　　　shrills
The Cricket's song, in warmth increasing ever,
　　And seems to one in drowsiness half lost,
　　　　The Grasshopper's among some grassy hills.

JOHN KEATS,
"On the Grasshopper and Cricket"

I

When lilacs last in the dooryard bloom'd,
And the great star early droop'd in the western sky in
    the night,
I mourn'd, and yet shall mourn with ever-returning
    spring.

Ever-returning spring, trinity sure to me you bring,
Lilac blooming perennial and drooping star in the
    west,
And thought of him I love.

II

O powerful western fallen star!
O shades of night—O moody, tearful night!
O great star disappear'd—O the black murk that hides
    the star!
O cruel hands that hold me powerless—O helpless
    soul of me!
O harsh surrounding cloud that will not free my soul.

III

In the dooryard fronting an old farm-house near the
    white-wash'd palings,
Stands the lilac-bush tall-growing with heart-shaped
    leaves of rich green,
With many a pointed blossom rising delicate, with the
    perfume strong I love,
With every leaf a miracle—and from this bush in the
    dooryard,

With delicate-color'd blossoms and heart-shaped
    leaves of rich green,
A sprig with its flower I break.

IV

In the swamp in secluded recesses,
A shy and hidden bird is warbling a song.

Solitary the thrush,
The hermit withdrawn to himself; avoiding the
    settlements,
Sings by himself a song.

Song of the bleeding throat,
Death's outlet song of life, (for well dear brother I
    know,
If thou wast not granted to sing thou would'st surely
    die.)

WALT WHITMAN,
from "When lilacs last in the dooryard bloom'd"

From too much love of living,
From hope and fear set free,
We thank with brief thanksgiving
Whatever gods may be
That no life lives forever;
That dead men rise up never;
That even the weariest river
Winds somewhere safe to sea.

ALGERNON CHARLES SWINBURNE,
from "The Garden of Proserpine"

Not every man has gentians in his house
in Soft September, at slow, sad Michaelmas.

Bavarian gentians, big and dark, only dark
darkening the day-time torch-like with the smoking
    blueness of Pluto's gloom,
ribbed and torch-like, with their blaze of darkness
    spread blue
down flattening into points, flattened under the sweep
    of white day
torch-flower of the blue-smoking darkness, Pluto's
    dark-blue daze,
black lamps from the halls of Dio, burning dark
    blue,
giving off darkness, blue darkness, as Demeter's pale
    lamps give off light,
lead me then, lead me the way.

Reach me a gentian, give me a torch!
let me guide myself with the blue, forked torch of this
    flower
down the darker and darker stairs, where blue is
    darkened on blueness
even where Persephone goes, just now, from the
    frosted September
to the sightless realm where darkness is awake upon
    the dark
and Persephone herself is but a voice
or a darkness invisible enfolded in the deeper dark
of the arms Plutonic, and pierced with the passion of
    dense gloom,

among the splendour of torches of darkness, shedding
   darkness on the lost bride and her groom.

D. H. LAWRENCE, "Bavarian Gentians"

Fergus. This whole day have I followed in the rocks,
   And you have changed and flowed from shape to
      shape,
   First as a raven on whose ancient wings
   Scarcely a feather lingered, then you seemed
   A weasel moving on from stone to stone,
   And now at last you wear a human shape,
   A thin grey man half lost in gathering night.

Druid. What would you, Fergus?

Fergus. Be no more a king
   But learn the dreaming wisdom that is yours.

Druid. Look on my thin grey hair and hollow cheeks
   And on these hands that may not lift the sword,
   This body trembling like a wind-blown reed.
   No woman's loved me, no man sought my help.

Fergus. A king is but a foolish labourer
   Who wastes his blood to be another's dream.

Druid. Take, if you must, this little bag of dreams;
   Unloose the cord, and they will wrap you round.

Fergus. I see my life go drifting like a river
   From change to change; I have been many things,

A green drop in the surge, a gleam of light
Upon a sword, a fir-tree on a hill,
An old slave grinding at a heavy quern,
A king sitting upon a chair of gold,
And all these things were wonderful and great;
But now I have grown nothing, knowing all.
Ah! Druid, Druid, how great webs of sorrow
Lay hidden in the small slate-coloured thing!

W. B. YEATS, from "Fergus and the Druid"

Stop searching stop weeping
she has gone to Heart Island

where the Truth People live
eating fern-shoots & berries

where there is no fighting
no sin no greed no sorrow.

JAMES LAUGHLIN, "Heart Island"

[T]he greatest confluence of all is that which makes
up the human memory—the individual human memory. My own is the treasure most dearly regarded by
me, in my life and in my work as a writer. Here time,
also, is subject to confluence. The memory is a living
thing—it too is in transit. But during its moment, all
that is remembered joins, and lives—the old and the
young, the past and the present, the living and the
dead.

EUDORA WELTY, from *One Writer's Beginnings*

What she made in her body is broken.
Now she has begun to bear it again.
In the house of her son's death
  his life is shining in the windows,
  for she has elected to bear him again.
  She did not bear him for death,
  and she does not. She has taken back
  into her body the seed, bitter
  and joyous, of the life of a man.

.   .   .

She did not bear him for death, and she does not.
There was a life that went out of her to live
on its own, divided, and now she has taken it back.
She is alight with the sudden new life of death.
Perhaps it is the brightness of the dead one
being born again. Perhaps she is planting him,
like corn, in the living and in the earth.
She has taken back into her flesh,
and made light, the dark seed of her pain.

                    WENDELL BERRY, from "Poem for J."

Autumn teaches us that fruition is also death; that
ripeness is a form of decay. The willows, having stood
for so long near water, begin to rust. Leaves are verbs
that conjugate the seasons.

   Today the sky is a wafer. Placed on my tongue, it is a
wholeness that has already disintegrated; placed under
the tongue, it makes my heart beat strongly enough to
stretch myself over the winter brilliances to come. Now
I feel the tenderness to which this season rots. Its de-

fenselessness can no longer be corrupted. Death is its purity, its sweet mud. The string of storms that came across Wyoming like elephants tied tail to trunk falters now and bleeds into a stillness.

There is neither sun, nor wind, nor snow falling. The hunters are gone; snow geese waddle in grainfields. Already, the elk have started moving out of the mountains toward sheltered feed-grounds. Their great antlers will soon fall off like chandeliers shaken from ballroom ceilings. With them the light of these autumn days, bathed in what Tennyson called "a mockery of sunshine," will go completely out.

GRETEL EHRLICH,
from *The Solace of Open Spaces*

Let the light of late afternoon
shine through chinks in the barn, moving
up the bales as the sun moves down.

Let the cricket take up chafing
as a woman takes up her needles
and her yarn. Let evening come.

Let dew collect on the hoe abandoned
in long grass. Let the stars appear
and the moon disclose her silver horn.

Let the fox go back to its sandy den.
Let the wind die down. Let the shed
go black inside. Let evening come.

To the bottle in the ditch, to the scoop
in the oats, to air in the lung
let evening come.

Let it come, as it will, and don't
be afraid. God does not leave us
comfortless, so let evening come.

JANE KENYON,
"Let Evening Come"

The art of losing isn't hard to master;
so many things seem filled with the intent
to be lost that their loss is no disaster.

Lose something every day. Accept the fluster
of lost door keys, the hour badly spent.
The art of losing isn't hard to master.

Then practice losing farther, losing faster:
places, and names, and where it was you meant
to travel. None of these will bring disaster.

I lost my mother's watch. And look! my last, or
next-to-last, of three loved houses went.
The art of losing isn't hard to master.

I lost two cities, lovely ones. And, vaster,
some realms I owned, two rivers, a continent.
I miss them, but it wasn't a disaster.

—Even losing you (the joking voice, a gesture
I love) I shan't have lied. It's evident
the art of losing's not too hard to master
though it may look like (*Write* it!) like disaster.

ELIZABETH BISHOP, "One Art"

The silence is vast
I am still and wander
Keeping you in mind
There is never enough
Time to know another

SAMUEL MENASHE, from "The Bare Tree"

Yes, they are alive, and can have those colors,
But I, in my soul, am alive too.
I feel I must sing and dance, to tell
Of this in a way, that knowing you may be drawn to
   me.

And I sing amid despair and isolation
Of the chance to know you, to sing of me
Which are you. You see,
You hold me up to the light in a way

I should never have expected, or suspected, perhaps
Because you always tell me I am you,
And right. The great spruces loom.
I am yours to die with, to desire.

I cannot ever think of me, I desire you
For a room in which the chairs ever
Have their backs turned to the light
Inflicted on the stone and paths, the real trees

That seem to shine at me through a lattice toward
    you
If the wild light of this January day is true
I pledge me to be truthful unto you
Whom I cannot ever stop remembering.

Remembering to forgive. Remember to pass beyond
    you into the day
On the wings of the secret you will never know
Taking me from myself, in the path
Which the pastel girth of the day has assigned to
    me.

I prefer "you" in the plural, I want "you,"
You must come to me, all golden and pale
Like the dew and the air.
And then I start getting this feeling of exaltation.

               JOHN ASHBERY, "A Blessing in Disguise"

Death flowing down past me, past me, death
marvelous, filthy, gold,
in my spine in my sex in my broken mouth
and the whole beautiful mouth of the child;
shedding power over me
death

if I acknowledge him.
Leading me
in my own body
at last in the dance.

MURIEL RUKEYSER,
from "The Sun-Artist"

Beauty is momentary in the mind—
The fitful tracing of a portal;
But in the flesh it is immortal.

The body dies; the body's beauty lives.
So evenings die, in their green going,
A wave, interminably flowing.

WALLACE STEVENS,
from "Peter Quince at the Clavier"

The ferry rocks us
out to the green sea
where man-o-wars slip,
perfect blue umbrellas
beneath us. Each seagull
dips and hangs—
and then is gone.

Look how everything passes:
each breath,
another gull is gone,
another man-o-war,

and so much sea,
this wrinkled blanket.
Our rocking's like
the moment before sleep.

We can't see the town yet.
There's nothing but this sea.
You sing a song:
o wie blüht mein Leib
aus jeder Ader.
Each seagull hangs.
The day is almost gone.

And all along we know
house lights on Friedrichskoog
are blinking on,
the swimmers are folding their towels,
and evening covers the town.
The body blooms, unfolding,
then is gone.

KEVIN PRUFER, "Returning to Friedrichskoog"

Healing, Changing,
Moving On

Perhaps much, perhaps sadly little, has been healed by the immediate circumstances of the ritual gathering, but as the service comes to an end, the company separates with, at least, a renewed sense of shared humanity. For each person henceforth, the mythologized "journey" goes forward toward whatever religious, philosophical, or imaginative insight lies ahead.

Stay together
learn the flowers
go light.

GARY SNYDER

Who would have thought my shrivell'd heart
Could have recovered greenness? It was gone
    Quite underground; as flowers depart
To see their mother-root, when they have blown;
        Where they together
        All the hard weather,
    Dead to the world, keep house unknown.

. . .

    And now in age I bud again,
After so many deaths I live and write;
    I once more smell the dew and rain,
And relish versing: O my only light,
        It cannot be
        That I am he
    On whom Thy tempests fell all night.

                    GEORGE HERBERT, from "The Flower"

Give me my Scallop shell of quiet,
My staffe of Faith to walke upon,
My Scrip of Joy, Immortall diet,
My bottle of salvation:
My Gowne of Glory, hopes true gage,
And thus Ile take my pilgrimage.

Blood must be my bodies balmer,
No other balme will there be given
Whilst my soule like a white Palmer
Travels to the land of heaven,
Over the silver mountaines,
Where spring the Nectar fountaines:
And there Ile kisse

The Bowle of blisse,
And drinke my eternall fill
On every milken hill.
My soule will be a drie before,
But after it, will nere thirst more.

And by the happie blisfull way
More peacefull Pilgrims I shall see,
That have shooke off their gownes of clay,

And goe appareld fresh like mee.
Ile bring them first
To slake their thirst,
And then to taste those Nectar suckets
At the cleare wells
Where sweetness dwells,
Drawne up by Saints in Christall buckets.

SIR WALTER RALEGH, from "The Passionate Mans
Pilgrimage," supposed to be written by one at the
point of death

Look homeward Angel now, and melt with ruth;
And, O ye Dolphins, waft the hapless youth.
   Weep no more, woeful Shepherds weep no more,
For Lycidas, your sorrow, is not dead,
Sunk though he be beneath the wat'ry floor,
So sinks the day-star in the ocean bed,
And yet anon repairs his drooping head,
And tricks his beams, and with new spangled ore,
Flames in the forehead of the morning sky

. . .

Readings for Remembrance

Now, Lycidas, the Shepherds weep no more;
Henceforth thou art the Genius of the shore,
In thy large recompense, and shalt be good
To all that wander in that perilous flood.
   Thus sang the uncouth Swain to th'oaks and rills,
While the still morn went out with sandals gray;

He touch'd the tender stops of various quills,
With eager thought warbling his Doric lay;
And now the sun had stretch'd out all the hills,
And now was dropped into the western bay;
At last he rose, and twitch'd his mantle blue;
To-morrow to fresh woods, and pastures new.

JOHN MILTON, from "Lycidas"

Dear to me is sleep: still more, being made of stone,
While pain and guilt still linger here below,
Blindness and numbness—these please me alone;
Then do not wake me, keep your voices low.

MICHELANGELO BUONARROTI,
"Dear to Me Is Sleep"

Of the dark past
A child is born
With joy and grief
My heart is torn

Calm in his cradle
The living lies.
May love and mercy
Unclose his eyes!

Young life is breathed
On the glass;
The world that was not
Comes to pass.

A child is sleeping:
An old man gone.
O, father forsaken,
Forgive your son!

JAMES JOYCE, "Ecce Puer"

Every person who makes us suffer we can associate with a divinity, of which that person is only a fragmentary reflexion—the lowest step of the approach to the temple, as it were—and the contemplation of this divinity as a pure idea gives us instant joy in place of the sorrow we were suffering; the entire art of living consists in making use of those who cause us suffering only as so many steps enabling us to draw nearer to its divine form and thus daily people our life with divinities.

MARCEL PROUST, from *The Past Recaptured*,
translation by Frederick A. Blossom

Do you think it is easy to change?
Ah, it is very hard to change and be different.
It means passing through the waters of oblivion.

D. H. LAWRENCE, "Change"

May my soul go out to the place which it desires without being imprisoned . . .

Inscription on twelfth-century Egyptian stela

At the last, tenderly,
From the walls of the powerful, fortressed house,
From the clasp of the knitted locks, from the keep of
   the well-closed doors,
Let me be wafted.

Let me glide noiselessly forth;
With the keys of softness unlock the locks—with a
   whisper
Set ope the doors O soul.

Tenderly—be not impatient,
(Strong is your hold O mortal flesh,
Strong is your hold O love.)

WALT WHITMAN,
"The Last Invocation," from Leaves of Grass

In this sad world of ours, sorrow comes to all.

. . .

Perfect relief is not possible, except with time.

You cannot now realize that you will ever feel better.
　　　And yet this is a mistake.
　　　You are sure to be happy again.
　　To know this, which is certainly true,
　　　will make you less miserable now.
　　I have experienced enough to know what I say.

ABRAHAM LINCOLN

I sing of autumn and the falling fruit
and the long journey towards oblivion.

The apples falling like great drops of dew
to bruise themselves an exit from themselves.

Have you built your ship of death, oh, have you?
Build then your ship of death, for you will need it!
.　　.　　.

thrust out onto the grey grey beaches of shadow
the long marginal stretches of existence, crowded with
　　lost souls
that intervene between our tower and the shaking sea
　　of the beyond.

Oh build your ship of death, oh build it in time
and build it lovingly, and put it between the hands of
　　your soul.

Over the sea, over the farthest sea
on the longest journey
past the jutting rocks of shadow
past the lurking, octopus arms of agonised memory

past the strange whirlpools of remembered greed
through the dead weed of a life-time's falsity,
slow, slow my soul, in his little ship
on the most soundless of all seas
taking the longest journey.

. . .

Drift on, drift on, my soul, towards the most pure
most dark oblivion.
And at the penultimate porches, the dark-red mantle
of the body's memories slips and is absorbed
into the shell-like, womb-like convoluted shadow.

And round the great final bend of unbroken dark
the skirt of the spirit's experience has melted away
the oars have gone from the boat, and the little dishes
gone, gone, and the boat dissolves like pearl
as the soul at last slips perfect into the goal, the core
of sheer oblivion and of utter peace

. . .

Oh build your ship of death
oh build it!
Oh, nothing matters but the longest journey.

D. H. LAWRENCE,
from "Ship of Death"

I turn my head and look towards death now.
Feeling my way through the tunnel with the space of
emptiness and quiet.
That shimmering silence that awaits me.
This is my direction now; inward to the
green pastures. . . .

The cares of the world concern me no longer.
I have completed this life. My work is done, my
children grown.
My husband is well on his hero's journey.
I have loved much and well. . . .
Those I leave behind, I love.
I hope I will remain in their hearts as they will
in mine . . .
Thank you for taking such good care of me. . . .
And all of you who have been my friends, thank you
for teaching me about love.

KAREN VERVAET,
from "Karen's Journal, 3 April 1993"

At the edge
Of a world
Beyond my eyes
Beautiful
I know Exile
Is always
Green with hope—
The river
We cannot cross
Flows forever

SAMUEL MENASHE, "Promised Land"

As with other children, when I was very young, death
was interesting—dead insects, dead birds, dead people.
In a middle-class, upper-middle-class milieu, everything connected to real death was odd, I mean in rela-

tion to pretensions and statements, projects and language and pride. Death seemed softly adamant, an undoing, a rearrangement, a softly meddlesome and irresistible silence. It was something some boys I knew and I thought we ought to familiarize ourselves with. Early on, and also in adolescence, we had a particular, conscious will not to be controlled by fear of death — there were things we would rather die than do. To some extent this rebelliousness was controlled; to some extent, we could choose our dangers, but not always. All this may be common among the young during a war; I grew up during the Second World War, when confronting unnatural death became a sad routine. . . .

It's my turn to die now — I can see that that is interesting to some people but not that it is tragic. . . .

I don't want to praise death, but in immediacy death confers a certain beauty on one's hours — a beauty that may not resemble any other sort but that is overwhelming. . . .

I believe that in the end it is sorrow over the world and over being disbelieved that kills us. It is the recognition of one's actual truth, the truth of one's actual life, that is so life-giving. . . .

At times I cannot entirely believe I ever was alive, that I ever was another self, and wrote — and loved or failed to love. I do not really understand this erasure. Oh, I can comprehend a shutting down, a great power replacing me with someone else (and with silence), but this inability to have an identity in the face of death — I don't believe I ever saw this written about in all the death scenes I have read or in all the descriptions of old age. It is curious how my life has tumbled to this point, how my memories no longer apply to the body in which my words are formed.

Perhaps you could say I did very little with my life, but the *douceur,* if that is the word, Talleyrand's word, was overwhelming. Painful and light-struck and wonderful. . . .

I don't know if the darkness is growing inward or if I am dissolving, softly exploding outward, into constituent bits in other existences: micro-existence. I am sensible of the velocity of the moments, and entering the part of my head alert to the motion of the world I am aware that life was never perfect, never absolute. This bestows contentment, even a fearlessness. Separation, detachment, death. I look upon another's insistence on the merits of his or her life—duties, intellect, accomplishment—and see that most of it is nonsense. And me, hell, I am a genius or I am a fraud, or—as I really think—I am possessed by voices and events from the earliest edge of memory and have never existed except as an Illinois front yard where these things play themselves out over and over again until I die. . . .

The world still seems far away. And I hear each moment whisper as it slides along. And yet I am happy—even overexcited, quite foolish. But *happy.* It seems very strange to think one could enjoy one's death. Ellen has begun to laugh at this phenomenon. We know we are absurd, but what can we do? We are happy. . . .

I am standing on an unmoored raft, a punt moving on the flexing, flowing face of a river. It is precarious. The unknowing, the taut balance, the jolts and the instability spread in widening ripples through all my thoughts.

Peace? There was never any in the world. But in the pliable water, under the sky, unmoored, I am traveling now and hearing myself laugh, at first with nerves and then with genuine amazement. It is all around me.

HAROLD BRODKEY, from *This Wild Darkness*

. . . I have walked through many lives,
some of them my own,
and I am not who I was,
though some principle of being
abides, from which I struggle
not to stray.
When I look behind,
as I am compelled to look
before I can gather strength
to proceed on my journey,
I see the milestones dwindling
toward the horizon
and the slow fires trailing
from the abandoned camp-sites,
over which scavenger angels
wheel on heavy wings.
Oh I have made myself a tribe
out of my true affections,
and my tribe is scattered!
How shall the heart be reconciled
to its feast of losses?
In a rising wind
the manic dust of my friends,
those who fell along the way,
bitterly stings my face.

Yet I turn, I turn,
exulting somewhat,
with my will intact to go
wherever I need to go,
and every stone on the road
precious to me.
In my darkest night,
when the moon was covered
and I roamed through wreckage,
a nimbus-clouded voice
directed me:
"Live in the layers,
not on the litter."
Though I lack the art
to decipher it,
no doubt the next chapter
in my book of transformations
is already written.
I am not done with my changes.

                    STANLEY KUNITZ, from "The Layers"

You were always changing into something else,
and always will be,
always plumage, perfection's broken heart, wings.

                                    FRANK O'HARA

Half-asleep again myself, I have a feeling of floating
down the river, and watching all the rubbish from the
house and from our lives—the good as well as the
bad—sinking slowly down through the dark water un-

til it is lost in the depths. Iris is floating or swimming quietly beside me. Weeds and larger leaves sway and stretch themselves beneath the surface. Blue dragon-flies dart and hover to and fro by the riverbank. And suddenly, a kingfisher flashes past.

JOHN BAYLEY, from *Elegy for Iris*

I can't tell if the day is ending, or the world,
or if the secret of secrets is within me again.

ANNA AKHMATOVA

I am going up stream
taking to the water from time to time
my marks dry off the stones before morning
the dark surface
strokes the night
above its way
There are no stars
there is no grief
I will never arrive
I stumble when I remember how it was
with one foot
one foot still in a name . . .

—————

When I stop I am alone
at night sometimes it is almost good
as though I were almost there
sometimes then I see there is
in a bush beside me the same question
why are you

on this way
I said I will ask the stars
why are you falling and they answered
which of us . . .

———

Maybe I will come
to where I am one
and find
I have been waiting there
as a new
year finds the song of the nuthatch

———

Send me out into another life
lord because this one is growing faint
I do not think it goes all the way

W. S. MERWIN,
from "Words for a Totem Animal"

Not every man knows what he shall sing at the end,
Watching the pier as the ship sails away, or what it
  will seem like
When he's held by the sea's roar, motionless, there at
  the end,
Or what he shall hope for once it is clear that he'll
  never go back.

When the time has passed to prune the rose or caress
  the cat, when
The sunset torching the lawn and the full moon icing it
  down

No longer appear, not every man knows what he'll
    discover instead,
When the weight of the past leans against nothing, and
    the sky

Is no more than remembered light, and the stories of
    cirrus
And cumulus come to a close, and all the birds are
    suspended in flight,
Not every man knows what is waiting for him, or what
    he shall sing
When the ship he is on slips into darkness, there at the
    end.

MARK STRAND, "The End"

1
It is no longer necessary to sleep
in order to dream of our destruction.

We take form within our death, the figures
emerging like shadows in fire.

Who is it? speaking to me of death's beauty.

I think it is my own black angel, as near me
as my flesh. I am never divided from his darkness.
His face is the black mask of my face. My eyes
live in his black eye-holes. On his black wings
I rise to sing.
            His mouthing presences attend

my singing, masquerading his black ambiguous
absolute:
       Die more lightly than live,
they say. Death is more gay.
                  There's no argument
against its certainty, at least, they say.

I know they know as surely as I live my death
exists, and has my shape.

2
But the man so forcefully walking,
say where he goes,
say what he hears and what he sees
and what he knows
to cause him to stride so merrily.

He goes in spring
through the evening street
to buy bread,

green trees leaning
over the sidewalk,
forsythia yellow
beneath the windows,
birds singing
as birds sing
only in spring,

and he sings, his footsteps
beating the measure of his song.

In an open window
a man and a woman
leaning together
at the room's center
embrace and kiss
as if they met
in passing,
the spring wind
lifting the curtain.

His footsteps carry him
past the window,
deeper into his song.

His singing becomes conglomerate
of all he sees,
leaving the street behind him
runged as a ladder
or the staff of a song.

3
To his death? Yes.

He walks and sings to his death.

And winter will equal spring.

And for the lovers, even
while they kiss, even though
it is spring, the day ends.

But to the sound of his passing
he sings. It is a kind of triumph
that he grieves — thinking
of the white lilacs in bloom,
profuse, fragrant, white
in excess of all seasonal need,

and of the mockingbird's crooked
arrogant notes, hooking him to the sky
as though no flight
or dying could equal him
at his momentary song.

WENDELL BERRY, "A Man Walking and
Singing: For James Baker Hall"

This singing
is a kind of dying,
a kind of birth,
a votive candle.
I have a dream-mother
who sings with her guitar,
nursing the bedroom
with moonlight and beautiful olives.
A flute came too,
joining the five strings,
a God finger over the holes.
I knew a beautiful woman once
who sang with her fingertips
and her eyes were brown
like small birds.
At the cup of her breasts

I drew wine.
At the mound of her legs
I drew figs.
She sang for my thirst,
mysterious songs of God
that would have laid an army down.
It is as if a morning-glory
had bloomed in her throat
and all that blue
and small pollen
ate into my heart
violent and religious.

ANNE SEXTON,
"The Fury of Guitars and Sopranos"

Now the washed sheets fly in the sun,
The pillow cases are sweetening.

It is a blessing, it is a blessing:
The long coffin of soap-colored oak,

The curious bearers and the raw date
Engraving itself in silver with marvelous calm.

SYLVIA PLATH, from "Berck-Plage"

Do not imagine you can abdicate   Auden

Prologue

If the sea could dream, and if the sea
were dreaming now, the dream
would be the usual one: Of the Flesh.
The letter written in the dream would go
something like: *Forgive me—love, Blue.*

I. The Viewing (A Chorus)

O what, then, did he look like?
                                    He had a good body.
And how came you to know this?
                                         His body was naked.
Say the sound of his body.
                                    His body was quiet.
Say again—quiet?
                              He was sleeping.
You are sure of this? Sleeping?
                                         Inside it, yes. Inside it.

.   .   .

III. The Tasting (A Chorus)

O what, then, did he taste like?
                                    He tasted of sorrow.
And how came you to know this?
                                    My tongue still remembers.
Say the taste that is sorrow.
                              Game, fallen unfairly.

And yet, you still tasted?

                        Still, I tasted.

Did you say to him something?

                    I could not speak, for hunger.

. . .

V. The Dreaming (A Chorus)

O what, then, did it feel like?

                  I dreamed of an arrow.

And how came you to know him?

                   I dreamed he was wanting.

Say the dream of him wanting.

               A swan, a wing folding.

Why do you weep now?

              I remember.

. . .

  Envoi

And I came to where was nothing but drowning
and more drowning, and saw to where the sea—
besides flesh—was, as well, littered with boats,
how each was blue but trimmed with white, to each
a name I didn't know and then, recalling,
did. And ignoring the flesh that, burning, gives
more stink than heat, I dragged what boats I could
to the shore and piled them severally in a treeless space, and lit a fire that didn't take
at first—the wood was wet—and then, helped by
the wind, became a blaze so high the sea
itself, along with the bodies in it, seemed

to burn. I watched as each boat fell to flame:
Vincent and *Matthew* and, last, what bore your name.

CARL PHILLIPS, from "Cortège"

Now that I have your face by heart, I look
Less at its features than its darkening frame
Where quince and melon, yellow as young flame,
Lie with quilled dahlias and the shepherd's crook.
Beyond, a garden. There, in insolent ease
The lead and marble figures watch the show
Of yet another summer loath to go
Although the scythes hang in the apple trees.

Now that I have your face by heart, I look.

Now that I have your voice by heart, I read
In the black chords upon a dulling page
Music that is not meant for music's cage,
Whose emblems mix with words that shake and bleed.
The staves are shuttled over with a stark
Unprinted silence. In a double dream
I must spell out the storm, the running stream.
The beat's too swift. The notes shift in the dark.

Now that I have your voice by heart, I read.

Now that I have your heart by heart, I see
The wharves with their great ships and architraves;
The rigging and the cargo and the slaves
On a strange beach under a broken sky.
O not departure, but a voyage done!
The bales stand on the stone; the anchor weeps
Its red rust downward, and the long vine creeps
Beside the salt herb, in the lengthening sun.

Now that I have your heart by heart, I see.

LOUISE BOGAN, "Song for the Last Act"

She had slept in the chair, like a passenger who had come on an emergency journey in a train. But she had rested deeply.

She had dreamed that she *was* a passenger, and riding with Phil. They had ridden together over a long bridge.

Awake, she recognized it: it was a dream of something that had really happened. When she and Phil were coming down from Chicago to Mount Salus to be married in the Presbyterian Church, they came on the train. Laurel, when she travelled back and forth between Mount Salus and Chicago, had always taken the sleeper. She and Phil followed the route on the day train, and she saw it for the first time.

When they were climbing the long approach to a bridge after leaving Cairo, rising slowly higher until they rode above the tops of bare trees, she looked down and saw the pale light widening and the river bottoms opening out, and then the water appearing, reflecting the low, early sun. There were two rivers. Here was where they came together. This was the confluence of the waters, the Ohio and the Mississippi.

They were looking down from a great elevation and all they saw was at the point of coming together, the bare trees marching in from the horizon, the rivers moving into one, and as he touched her arm she looked up with him and saw the long, ragged, pencil-faint line of birds within the crystal of the zenith, flying in a V of their own, following the same course down. All they could see was sky, water, birds, light, and confluence. It was the whole morning world.

And they themselves were a part of the confluence. Their own joint act of faith had brought them here at the very moment and matched its occurrence, and proceeded as it proceeded. Direction itself was made beautiful, momentous. They were riding as one with it, right up front. It's our turn! she'd thought exultantly. And we're going to live forever.

Left bodiless and graveless of a death made of water and fire in a year long gone, Phil could still tell her of her life. For her life, any life, she had to believe, was nothing but the continuity of its love.

EUDORA WELTY, from *The Optimist's Daughter*

I love the dark hours of my being
in which my senses drop into the deep.
I have found in them as in old letters,
my private life, that is already lived through,

and become wide and powerful now, like legend.
Then I know that there is room in me
for a huge and timeless life.

RAINER MARIA RILKE,
translation by Robert Bly

It's a strange courage
you give me ancient star:

Shine alone in the sunrise
toward which you lend no part!

WILLIAM CARLOS WILLIAMS, "El Hombre"

it will not be simple, it will not be long
it will take little time, it will take all your thought
it will take all your heart, it will take all your breath
it will be short, it will not be simple

it will touch through your ribs, it will take all your
     heart
it will not be long, it will occupy your thought
as a city is occupied, as a bed is occupied
it will take all your flesh, it will not be simple

You are coming into us who cannot withstand you
you are coming into us who never wanted to withstand
     you
you are taking parts of us into places never planned
you are going far away with pieces of our lives

it will be short, it will take all your breath
it will not be simple, it will become your will

ADRIENNE RICH, "Final Notations"

"If I died, what would you do?" I asked him long ago.
And he told me, "I would have my time of mourning.
That would be slow and very hard. But there would
come a time when I would look at myself and say,
'Well, what kind of life do you want now? In what direction will you go?' It would be the death of a part of
me. But listen, Martha: There would never be a question of my not surviving. *Never.*"

Hal. *L'chaim.*

MARTHA WEINMAN LEAR, from *Heartsounds*

The palm at the end of the mind,
Beyond the last thought, rises
In the bronze decor,

A gold-feathered bird
Sings in the palm, without human meaning,
Without human feeling, a foreign song.

You know then that it is not the reason
That makes us happy or unhappy.
The bird sings. Its feathers shine.

The palm stands on the edge of space.
The wind moves slowly in the branches.
The bird's fire-fangled feathers dangle down.

WALLACE STEVENS, "Of Mere Being"

I danced in the morning when the world was begun,
And I danced in the moon and the stars and the sun,
And I came down from heaven and I danced on the
   earth,
At Bethlehem I had my birth.

[Refrain:]
Dance then, wherever you may be,
I am the Lord of the Dance said he,
And I'll lead you all wherever you may be,
And I'll lead you all in the Dance said he.

. . .

I danced on a Friday when the sky turned black.
It's hard to dance with the devil on your back.
They buried my body and they thought I'd gone,
But I am the dance and I still go on.

[Refrain:]
They cut me down and I leap up high.
I am the life that'll never die.
I'll live in you if you'll live in me.
I am the Lord of the Dance, said he.

from "Lord of the Dance" (folksong)

Suggested Readings for Friends and Family

Lines from almost any selection in this volume could be read for any subject depending on the reader's emotional tie to the deceased. Here are a few particularly appropriate ones:

Remembering a father:

16 Michel de Montaigne, from *The Autobiography*
24 Walter Savage Landor, "Finis"
26 Constance Egemo, "The Gathering"
65 Dylan Thomas, "Do not go gentle into that good night"

Remembering a mother:

36 Saint Augustine, from "On the Death of His Mother"
80 Rainer Maria Rilke, from "Requiem"
84 T. S. Eliot, from "Little Gidding"
87 Theodore Roethke, from "The Lost Son"

Remembering a husband:

34 Homer, from *The Odyssey*
107 Lady Catherine Dyer, "My Dearest Dust"
116 William Carlos Williams, "The Widow's Lament in Springtime"
140 William Penn, from "Union of Friends"

Remembering a wife:

56 Thomas Hardy, from "The Walk"
56 Thomas Hardy, from "The Voice"
115 Rudyard Kipling, "The Widower"
121 Winston Churchill, from a letter to his wife

Remembering a child:

43 Anne Bradstreet, from "In Memory of . . ."
43 Walter de la Mare, "Even in the Grave"
44 Ralph Waldo Emerson, from "Threnody"
53 William Blake, "On Another's Sorrow"
64 James Laughlin, "Are You Still Alone"
125 Nancy Dingman Watson, "you came to me"
176 Wendell Berry, from "Poem for J."

Remembering a sister:

19 Emily Dickinson, "The bustle in a house"
25 Li Po, "Lady Wang-Chao—II"
94 Sappho, "Epitaph"

Remembering a brother:

20 Leo Tolstoy, from *What Men Live By*
23 Walt Whitman, from "A Clear Midnight"
49 Kenneth Rexroth, AKAHITO (V), and THE EMPRESS
   YAMATOHIME (XCIX)
77 Leigh Hunt, from a letter on the death of John Keats

Remembering an honored elder:

67 Annie Dillard, from *The Living*
77 John Stuart Mill

78 Albert Einstein, from a letter on the death of physicist M. Besso

117 Henry Wadsworth Longfellow, from "A Psalm of
Life"

117 William Johnson-Cory, "Heraclitus"

Remembering a beloved friend:

17 Samuel Johnson, from *The Letters*

17, 186 John Milton, from "Lycidas"

20 George Gordon, Lord Byron, "So, We'll Go No
More A-Roving"

21 A. E. Housman, "We'll to the Woods No More"

21 John Hollander, "An Old-Fashioned Song"

37 Saint Augustine, from "On the Death of a Friend"

152 Percy Bysshe Shelley, from "Adonais"

181 Kevin Prufer, "Returning to Friedrichskoog"

189 Walt Whitman, "The Last Invocation," from *Leaves
of Grass*

Suggestions for Music

It seems altogether natural to the human ear to interpret musical sounds as expressive of strong emotion. Indeed, in time of sorrow, music may say what the heart finds no words for. For this reason, the evocative power of a memorial service can depend very much on the choice of musical selections and instruments, voice, or chorus to perform them. Music can be interspersed among eulogies and scriptural readings, or it can provide quiet background while the participants find their seats.

Religious counselors are ready to help families put together such a service. Formal services often include well-rehearsed performances of sections of works by Bach, Mozart, Brahms, Schubert, Schumann, Mahler, and other canonical composers. For less formal services, a single flutist, pianist, guitarist, or vocalist offering folk songs or even songs from the vast popular repertoire add to the event. Or tapes can be used in one's home (any recording by the Tallis Scholars, who specialize in medieval choral music, would be fitting). In any case, a cornucopia of selections exists for performance by professional or amateur musicians, members of a local chamber music group, or a single performer. There is even precedent for the playing of bagpipes at a funeral. The pipes were traditionally played in Scotland, Ireland, and the Celtic diaspora "to accompany the dead to the grave, making such mournful sounds as to invite, nay almost force, the bystanders to weep." So wrote a sixteenth-century traveler. Today, some local police and fire departments can recommend available pipers. In all these circumstances, it is helpful to have a printed program announcing composer and titles and, where appropriate, the texts of hymns.

Here, in no particular order of suitability, are a number of selections I've collected from services formal and informal and with the advice of music specialists:

BACH

Sonata No. 3 in E Major for violin and piano (3rd movement)

Air from Suite No. 3 in D Major (BWV 1069)

Concerto in D for two violins (2nd movement)

The Ascension Oratorio, Cantata No. 11 ("Ah! Stay a while, my most sweet life / Ah! flee not so soon from me!")

"Vor deinen Thron tret' ich"

Mass in B Minor (Agnus Dei)

St. John Passion (final chorale)

"Komm, Jesu, komm!" (final chorale)

"Jesu Joy of Man's Desiring" (from Cantata BWV 147)

SAMUEL BARBER

Adagio from *Quartet for Strings*

"Three Songs" (setting for poems by James Agee, James Stephens, and a translation of a medieval work by W. H. Auden)

BEETHOVEN
Funeral March from Symphony No. 3 in E-flat Major, op. 55

BRAHMS
Requiem (final movement)

CHOPIN
Funeral March from Piano Sonata No. 2 in B-flat Minor, op. 35
Preludes, op. 28

AARON COPLAND
"Three Songs" (setting for poems by Emily Dickinson and Robert Lowry, and a Shaker poem)

DURUFLÉ
Requiem (selections)

FAURÉ
Requiem, op. 48 ("In Paradisum," "Pie Jesu")

GLUCK
"Dance of the Blessed Spirits" from *Orfeo ed Euridice*

GRIEG
"Last Spring" from *Two Elegiac Melodies*, op. 34

CHARLES IVES
Symphony No. 3 (3rd movement)

ALONSO LOBO
   "Versa est in luctum"

MAHLER
   Das Lied von der Erde (settings for eighth-century Chi-
      nese poems, written after the death of his four-
      year-old daughter)
   Kindertotenlieder (songs on the death of children)
   Symphony No. 2, "Resurrection" (1st movement)

MENDELSSOHN
   Quartet No. 6 in F Minor for strings ("for the dead
      Fanny")

MOZART
   Clarinet Concerto (2nd movement)
   Exsultate Jubilate! from *Solemn Vespers*
   Funeral Music in C Minor
   Requiem Mass (K. 626)
   Mass in C Minor (K. 427)

PURCELL
   Funeral Sentences "On the Death of Queen Mary"
      (Z. 860A)
   "Dido's Farewell," from *Dido and Aeneas*, Act III

RAVEL
   Kaddish

MARTIN ROKEACH
   Coda

NED ROREM
Evidence of Things Not Seen (cycle of thirty-six songs
set to poems by Paul Goodman, Whitman,
Wordsworth, Millay, Frost, Dickinson, and
others)

SCHUBERT
"An die Musik"
Piano Trio in B-flat, op. 99 (slow movement)
Piano Fantasy in F Minor for four hands
Octet for Winds and Strings in F Major, op. 166
(Adagio)
String Quartet in D Minor ("Death and the
Maiden")

SCHUMANN
Piano Quartet in E-flat Major, op. 47 (Andante)

JOHN TAVERNER
Funeral Ikos
Song for Athene

VAUGHN WILLIAMS
Oboe Concerto

BERNARD ALOIS ZIMMERMAN
Requiem for a Young Poet

Some hymn and song selections:

"Bang the Drum Slowly"
"Amazing Grace"

"Abide with Me"
"Simple Gifts" and other Shaker songs
Various settings for the 23rd Psalm (as, Mishkin:
    "We shall walk through the Valley")

Pop songs may have their place as well, played quietly
    by the right hands for the right listeners:

ERIC CLAPTON
    "Tears in Heaven" (after the death of his young son)

BOB DYLAN
    "Knocking on Heaven's Door"

TERRY JACKS
    "Seasons in the Sun"

ELTON JOHN
    "Candle in the Wind" (written for Princess Diana)

TINA TURNER
    "Simply the Best"

LED ZEPPELIN
    "Stairway to Heaven"

Index

ADAMS, HENRY
    from *History of the United States of America During the First
        Administration of Thomas Jefferson*, 121
Addison, Joseph (translator), 72
"Adonais: An Elegy on the Death of John Keats" (Shelley),
        45–46, 152–54
Aeneid, The (Virgil), 100
"After great pain" (Dickinson), 51
AKAHITO
    The mists rise over, 49
AKHMATOVA, ANNA
    I can't tell if the day is ending, 197
Alexander, Michael (translator), 101
All the Strange Hours (Eiseley), 62–63
All you who mourn the loss of loved ones (*The Union Prayerbook*),
        15–16
"Altar of the Dead, The" (James), 84
"Amazing Grace," 140–41
American Indian poems, 81
"And Then" (García Lorca), 68
"Anthem for Doomed Youth" (Owen), 58
Apology of Socrates, The (Plato), 71–72
ARENDT, HANNAH
    However much we are affected by the things of the
        world, 29
"Are You Still Alone" (Laughlin), 64
Ariès, Philippe, 3
ASHBERY, JOHN
    "A Blessing in Disguise," 179–80
AUDEN, W. H.
    "Funeral Blues," 57–58

AUGUSTINE, SAINT, 3–4
    from "On the Death of a Friend," 37–38
    from "On the Death of His Mother," 37
Autobiography, The (Montaigne), 16–17
Aztec poem, 81

Babbitt, Irving (translator), 142
BACHELARD, GASTON
    The only possible proof of the existence of water, 77
"Ballad of Dead Ladies, The" (Villon), 101–2
"Bare Tree, The" (Menashe), 179
"Bavarian Gentians" (Lawrence), 173–74
BAYLEY, JOHN
    from *Elegy for Iris*, 196–97
Be not curious about God (Whitman), 78
Beowulf (Alexander, translator), 101
"Berck-Plage" (Plath), 203
BERRY, WENDELL
    "A Man Walking and Singing: For James Baker Hall,"
      199–202
    from "Poem for J.," 176
Besso, M., Einstein's letter on, 78
BIBLE
    from Ecclesiastes, 137–38
    from Genesis, 131
    from Isaiah, 132
    from Matthew, 138
    from Psalms, 135–37
BISHOP, ELIZABETH
    "One Art," 178–79
BLACK ELK
    O Great Spirit, 139
Black Elk Speaks (Black Elk), 139
"Black Lamb, The" (Wilde), 85
BLAKE, WILLIAM
    "On Another's Sorrow," 53–55
"Blessing in Disguise, A" (Ashbery), 179–80
"Blessing of Women, A" (Kunitz), 110–11
Blossom, Frederick A. (translator), 121, 188
Bly, Robert (translator), 208–9

BOGAN, LOUISE
    "Song for the Last Act," 206–7
Book of Margins, The (Jabes), 79, 87
BOURDILLON, FRANCIS WILLIAM
    "Light," 57
BRADSTREET, ANNE
        from "In Memory of My Dear Grandchild Elizabeth
            Bradstreet, Who Deceased August, 1665, Being a Year
            and Half Old," 43
BRODKEY, HAROLD
        from *This Wild Darkness*, 192–95
brother, readings for remembering, 214
BUBER, MARTIN
        from "Here Where One Stands," 78–79
"Buddha in Glory" (Rilke), 157
Buddhist aphorism (Babbitt, translator), 142
"Buffalo Bill 's" (Cummings), 125
"Burial of Sir John Moore at Coruña, The" (Wolfe), 109–10
"Bustle in a house, the" (Dickinson), 19–20
But I claim (Sappho), 90
"By a Holm-Oak" (Smith), 60–61
BYRON, GEORGE GORDON, LORD
        "So, We'll Go No More A-Roving," 20–21

CALDERÓN
        Life is a dream, 70
"Canto CXIV" (Pound), 155
CATO
        from "Soliloquy on Immortality," 72
CATULLUS
        Over many lands and seas have I journeyed, 35
CAVAFY, C. P.
        "For Ammonis, Who Died at 29, in 610," 15
        from "The Horses of Achilles," 97
CELAN, PAUL
        "Death Fugue," 59–60
CERVANTES, MIGUEL DE
        from *Don Quixote*, 108–9
"Change" (Lawrence), 189
child, readings for remembering, 214

Index

CHUANG TZU
    from *Musings of a Chinese Mystic*, 75, 143–44
CHURCHILL, WINSTON
    Do not grieve for me too much, 121
Circle of Stones: A Woman's Journey to Herself (Duerk), 61–62
CLARE, JOHN
    "An Invite, to Eternity," 40–41
    "I Am," 41
"Clear Midnight, A" (Whitman), 23
Confessions, The (Augustine), 36–38
"Contemplation upon Flowers, A" (King), 162–63
"Cortège" (Phillips), 204–6
COWLEY, ABRAHAM
    from "On the Death of Mr. William Harvey," 108
"Crossing the Bar" (Tennyson), 166
CUMMINGS, E. E.
    "Buffalo Bill 's," 125
Cymbeline (Shakespeare), 167–68
"Cynthia's Reve" (Jonson), 42

DANTE
    from *The Divine Comedy: The Paradiso*, 138–39
"Dead, The" (Joyce), 52–53
"Dead in Europe, The" (Lowell), 58–59
"Dear to Me Is Sleep" (Michelangelo), 187
"Death, be not proud" (Donne), 152
"Death Fugue" (Celan), 59–60
Death of Adam, The (Robinson), 87
"Death of Enkidu, The" (Mason, translator), 91–92
"Death of Phaethon, The" (Ovid), 93–94
"Death of Stonewall Jackson, The" (Henderson), 114–15
Death speaks (Maugham), 82
DE LA MARE, WALTER
    "Even in the Grave," 43
Dhammapada, The, 142
DICKINSON, EMILY
    "After great pain," 51
    "The bustle in a house," 19–20
    "There's a certain slant of light," 19

Di Giovanni, Norman Thomas (translator), 68

DILLARD, ANNIE
    from *The Living*, 67–68

"Dirge," from *Cymbeline* (Shakespeare), 167–68

Divine Comedy, The: The Paradiso (Dante), 138–39

DONNE, JOHN
    "Death, be not proud," 152

"Do not go gentle into that good night" (Thomas), 65–66

Do not grieve for me too much (Churchill), 121

Don Quixote (Cervantes), 108–9

Down goes the river (spiritual), 61

Dream that my little baby came to life again (Wollstonecraft), 43

Dryden, John (translator), 74

DUERK, JUDITH
    from *Circle of Stones: A Woman's Journey to Herself*, 61–62

DUNBAR, WILLIAM
    from "Lament for the Makers," 38–39

DYER, LADY CATHERINE
    "My Dearest Dust," 107

"East Coker" (Eliot), 63

Eberhard, Otto (translator), 131

"Ecce Puer" (Joyce), 187–88

Ecclesiastes, 137–38

EGEMO, CONSTANCE
    "The Gathering," 26

Egyptian stela, inscription on, 189

EHRLICH, GRETEL
    from *The Solace of Open Spaces*, 176–77

EINSTEIN, ALBERT, 4
    In quitting this strange world, 78

EISELEY, LOREN
    from *All the Strange Hours*, 62–63

elder, honored, readings for remembering, 214

Elegy for Iris (Bayley), 196–97

"El Hombre" (Williams), 209

ELIOT, T. S.
    from "East Coker," 63
    from "Little Gidding," 84

EMERSON, RALPH WALDO, 2
    inscription for a well in memory of the martyrs of the
        war, 112
    from "Self Reliance," 112
    from "Threnody," 44–45
"End, The" (Strand), 198–99
EPICTETUS
    from *The Manual*, 74–75
"Epitaph" (Sappho), 94
Essay on Man, An (Pope), 163–64
"Eternal Goodness, The" (Whittier), 141
EURIPIDES
    There be many shapes of mystery, 14
"Evening Hymn" (Fuller), 162
"Even in the Grave" (de la Mare), 43
"Eventide" (Lyte), 156–57
Everyman, 161–62

Faerie Queen, The (Spenser), 162
"Fairy's Funeral, A" (North), 27–28
Fall, stream, from Heaven to bless (Emerson), 112
father, readings for remembering, 213
"Fergus and the Druid" (Yeats), 174–75
"Field Hospital, A" (Jarrell), 122–23
"Final Notations" (Rich), 209–10
"Finis" (Landor), 24
Finnegans Wake (Joyce), 53
Fitzgerald, Edward (translator), 165
"Flower, The" (Herbert), 185
"For Ammonis, Who Died at 29, in 610" (Cavafy), 15
"For J." (Garrigue), 127
FRANCIS OF ASSISI, SAINT
    from *The Mirror of Perfection*, 146–47
friend, readings for remembering, 215
"Friends Departed" (Vaughan), 151
"Friends of my father, the" (Menashe), 124
FROST, ROBERT
    "Nothing Gold Can Stay," 86
FUJIWARA NO TOSHINARI
    In all the world, 48

FULLER, WILLIAM
    "Evening Hymn," 162
"Funeral Blues" (Auden), 57–58
"Fury of Guitars and Sopranos, The" (Sexton), 202–3

GARCÍA LORCA, FEDERICO
    "And Then," 68
"Garden of Proserpine, The" (Swinburne), 172
GARRIGUE, JEAN
    "For J.," 127
"Gathering, The" (Egemo), 26
Genesis, 131
Gentle lady, do not sing (Joyce), 161
Giles, H. A., 144
Gilgamesh: A Verse Narrative (Mason, translator), 91–92
"Good-Night, A" (Quarles), 166
"Grace, A" (Hall), 65
Grandestine, Abbess of, 161

HALL, DONALD
    "A Grace," 65
Hamburger, Michael (translator), 59–60
Hamlet (Shakespeare), 106
HANAZONO, EMPEROR
    The servants, the pomp, have vanished, 48
HARDY, THOMAS
    from "The Voice," 56–57
    from "The Walk," 56
HAYDEN, ROBERT
    "Those Winter Sundays," 124
"Heart Island" (Laughlin), 175
Heartsounds (Lear), 210
Heidegger, Martin, 3
HENDERSON, GEORGE FRANCIS ROBERT
    "The Death of Stonewall Jackson," 114–15
Henry VIII (Shakespeare), 167
"Heraclitus" (Johnson-Cory), 117–18
HERBERT, GEORGE
    from "Man," 148–50

HERBERT, GEORGE (*cont.*)
    from "The Flower," 185
    "Virtue," 148
"Here Where One Stands" (Buber), 78–79
Hindu teachings (Mascaro, translator), 144–46
History of the Peloponnesian War (Thucydides), 97–100
History of the United States of America During the First Administration of
    Thomas Jefferson (Adams), 121
HOLLANDER, JOHN
    "An Old-Fashioned Song," 21–22
HOMER
    from *The Odyssey*, 34
honored elder, readings for remembering, 214
HOPKINS, GERARD MANLEY
    from "I wake and feel the fell of dark," 50
    from "No worst, there is none," 50
    "Pied Beauty," 139–40
    "Spring and Fall: To a Young Child," 18
HORACE
    Melpomene, teach me how to grieve, 35
HORIKAWA, EMPEROR
    Long, long since I saw the building of my beloved's house,
      48
"Horses of Achilles, The" (Cavafy), 97
HOUSMAN, A. E.
    "We'll to the Woods No More," 21
However much we are affected by the things of the world
    (Arendt), 29
Hughes, Ted (translator), 94
Human existence is girt round with mystery (Mill), 77
HUNT, LEIGH
    Tell him that we shall all bear his memory, 77–78
husband, readings for remembering, 213

"I Am" (Clare), 41
I can't tell if the day is ending (Akhmatova), 197
Idylls of the King (Tennyson), 102–4
I have suffered more than ever I thought I could (Tennyson),
    43
I love the dark hours of my being (Rilke), 208–9

"In a Dark Time" (Roethke), 66–67

In all the world (Fujiwara no Toshinari), 48

Indian poems, 81

"In Flanders Fields" (McCrae), 122

"In Memory of My Dear Grandchild Elizabeth Bradstreet, Who
       Deceased August, 1665, Being a Year and Half Old"
       (Bradstreet), 43

In quitting this strange world (Einstein), 78

"In the event of my death . . ." (Churchill), 121

In the great night my heart will go out (Papago poem), 81

In this sad world of ours, sorrow comes to all (Lincoln), 189–90

"In times when nothing stood" (Larkin), 127

"Invite, to Eternity, An" (Clare), 40–41

Isaiah, 132

"I wake and feel the fell of dark" (Hopkins), 50

JABES, EDMOND
    from *The Book of Margins*, 79, 87

JAMES, HENRY
    from *Notebook*, 83–84
    from "The Altar of the Dead," 84

Japanese poems, 48–49

JARRELL, RANDALL
    "A Field Hospital," 122–23

JOHNSON, SAMUEL
    from *The Letters*, 17

JOHNSON-CORY, WILLIAM
    "Heraclitus," 117–18

JONSON, BEN
    from "Cynthia's Reve," 42
    "On my first son," 42
    on Shakespeare, 106–7

Journal (Wordsworth), 22–23

Jowett, B. (translator), 72, 96

JOYCE, JAMES
    "Ecce Puer," 187–88
    from *Finnegans Wake*, 53
    Gentle lady, do not sing, 161
    from "The Dead," 52–53

Julius Caesar (Shakespeare), 76, 105

Kaddish, 133–34

"Karen's Journal, 3 April 1993" (Vervaet), 191–92

KEATS, JOHN
  Hunt's letter on, 77–78
  "On the Grasshopper and Cricket," 170

Keeley, Edmund, 15, 97

KENYON, JANE
  "Let Evening Come," 177–78

Kiesler, Frederick, 6

KING, HENRY
  from "A Contemplation upon Flowers," 162–63

KIPLING, RUDYARD
  "L'envoi," 156
  "The Widower," 115–16

KUNITZ, STANLEY
  from "A Blessing of Women," 110–11
  "The Layers," 195–96

Kurata, Ryukichi (translator), 47, 48

"Lady Wang-Chao—II" (Li Po), 25

"Lament for the Makers" (Dunbar), 38–39

LANDOR, WALTER SAVAGE
  "Finis," 24

LAO-TZU
  from *Tao Te Ching*, 143

LARKIN, PHILIP
  "In times when nothing stood," 127

"Last Invocation, The" (Whitman), 189

Latham, Ronald (translator), 73

Lattimore, Richmond (translator), 90, 94, 130

LAUGHLIN, JAMES
  "Are You Still Alone," 64
  "Heart Island," 175

LAWRENCE, D. H.
  "Bavarian Gentians," 173–74
  "Change," 189
  from "Ship of Death," 190–91

"Layers, The" (Kunitz), 195–96

LEAR, MARTHA WEINMAN
  from *Heartsounds*, 210

Leaves of Grass (Whitman), 189

"L'envoi" (Kipling), 156

"Let Evening Come" (Kenyon), 177–78

Letters, The (Johnson), 17

LEVINE, PHILIP
  from "On the Meeting of García Lorca and Hart Crane,"
    28–29

Lewis, Cecil Day (translator), 100

Life is a dream (Calderón), 70

"Light" (Bourdillon), 57

LINCOLN, ABRAHAM
  In this sad world of ours, sorrow comes to all, 189–90

"Lines Composed a Few Miles Above Tintern Abbey"
    (Wordsworth), 169–70

LI PO
  "Lady Wang-Chao — II," 25
  "On Seeing Off Meng Hao-Jan," 25

"Little Gidding" (Eliot), 84

Living, The (Dillard), 67–68

Long, long since I saw the building of my beloved's house
    (Emperor Horikawa), 48

LONGFELLOW, HENRY WADSWORTH
  from "A Psalm of Life," 117

"Lord of the Dance" (folksong), 211

"Lost Son, The" (Roethke), 87–88

Loveliest of what I leave behind is the sunlight (Praxílla of
    Sícyon), 130

LOWELL, ROBERT
  "The Dead in Europe," 58–59

Lowenthal, Marvin (translator), 17

LUCRETIUS
  from *On the Nature of the Universe*, 72–73

"Lycidas" (Milton), 17, 186–87

LYTE, HENRY FRANCIS
  "Eventide," 156–57

McCRAE, JOHN
  "In Flanders Fields," 122

"Man" (Herbert), 148–50

Mandelbaum, Allen, 139

Index   [233]

Manual, The (Epictetus), 74–75

"Man Walking and Singing, A: For James Baker Hall" (Berry), 199–202

"March in the Ranks Hard-Prest, and the Road Unknown, A" (Whitman), 112–14

MARCUS AURELIUS
    from *Meditations*, 75–76

Mascaro, J. (translator), 146

Mason, Herbert (translator), 92

Matthew, 138

MAUGHAM, W. SOMERSET
    Death speaks, 82

Maya poems, 81

Meditations (Marcus Aurelius), 75–76

Melpomene, teach me how to grieve (Horace), 35

Memoir of a Modernist's Daughter (Munro), 27

MENASHE, SAMUEL
    "Promised Land," 192
    from "The Bare Tree," 179
    "The friends of my father," 124

MERWIN, W. S.
    from "Words for a Totem Animal," 197–98

Metamorphoses (Ovid), 74

MICHELANGELO BUONARROTI
    "Dear to Me Is Sleep," 187

MILL, JOHN STUART
    Human existence is girt round with mystery, 77

MILLAY, EDNA ST. VINCENT
    "Time does not bring relief," 62

MILOSZ, CZESLAW
    from "On Parting with My Wife, Janina," 86

MILTON, JOHN
    from "Lycidas," 17, 186–87

Mirror of Perfection, The (Francis of Assisi), 146–47

Mitchell, Stephen (translator), 80, 157

MONTAIGNE, MICHEL DE, 1, 2
    from *The Autobiography*, 16–17

mother, readings for remembering, 213

MUNRO, ELEANOR
    from *Memoir of a Modernist's Daughter*, 27

music, 217–22

Musings of a Chinese Mystic (Chuang Tzu), 75, 143–44
"My Dearest Dust" (Dyer), 107
"Mysterious Tao, The" (Chuang Tzu), 75

NEWMAN, JOHN HENRY
    from "The Pillar of the Cloud," 141–42
Nietzsche, Friedrich, 7
"Night, The" (Vaughan), 152
NORTH, CHRISTOPHER (JOHN WILSON)
    from "A Fairy's Funeral," 27–28
Notebook (James), 83–84
"Nothing Gold Can Stay" (Frost), 86
Nothing that ever flew (author unknown), 86
"No worst, there is none" (Hopkins), 50

"Ode: Intimations of Immortality from Recollections of Early
        Childhood" (Wordsworth), 154–55
Odyssey, The (Homer), 34
Oedipus the King (Sophocles), 100
"Of Mere Being" (Stevens), 210–11
"O God, Our Help" (Watts), 142
O Great Spirit (Black Elk), 139
O'HARA, FRANK
    You were always changing into something else, 196
"Old-Fashioned Song, An" (Hollander), 21–22
Oldfather, W. A. (translator), 75
"On Another's Sorrow" (Blake), 53–55
"One Art" (Bishop), 178–79
One Writer's Beginnings (Welty), 175
"On my first son" (Jonson), 42
"On Parting with My Wife, Janina" (Milosz), 86
"On Seeing Off Meng Hao-Jan" (Li Po), 25
"On the Death of a Friend" (Augustine), 37–38
"On the Death of His Mother" (Augustine), 37
"On the Death of Mr. William Harvey" (Cowley), 108
"On the Grasshopper and Cricket" (Keats), 170
"On the Meeting of García Lorca and Hart Crane" (Levine),
        28–29
On the Nature of the Universe (Lucretius), 72–73

Optimist's Daughter, The (Welty), 207–8

Others may forget you (Empress Yamatohime), 49

Over many lands and seas have I journeyed (Catullus), 35

OVID

 from *Metamorphoses,* 74

 from "The Death of Phaethon," 93–94

OWEN, WILFRED

 "Anthem for Doomed Youth," 58

Papago poem, 81

PASCAL, BLAISE

 from *Pensées,* 77

"Passionate Mans Pilgrimage, The" (Ralegh), 185–86

Past Recaptured, The (Proust), 118–21, 188

PENN, WILLIAM

 from "Union of Friends," 140

Pensées (Pascal), 77

Perchance do we truly live on earth? (Aztec poem), 81

"Peter Quince at the Clavier" (Stevens), 181

Phaedo, The (Plato), 95–96

PHILLIPS, CARL

 from "Cortège," 204–6

"Pied Beauty" (Hopkins), 139–40

"Pillar of the Cloud, The" (Newman), 141–42

PLATH, SYLVIA

 from "Berck-Plage," 203

PLATO

 from *The Apology of Socrates,* 71–72

 from *The Phaedo,* 95–96

"Poem for J." (Berry), 176

POPE, ALEXANDER

 from *An Essay on Man,* 163–64

"Portrait (modelled after ee cummings)" (Watson), 125

POUND, EZRA, 2

 from "Canto CXIV," 155

PRAXÍLLA OF SÍCYON

 Loveliest of what I leave behind is the sunlight, 130

"Prayer for Osiris" (rendered by Eberhard), 131

"Promised Land" (Menashe), 192

PROUST, MARCEL
    from *The Past Recaptured*, 118–21, 188
Prufer, Kevin
    "Returning to Friedrichskoog," 181–82
"Psalm of Life, A" (Longfellow), 117
PSALMS
    from Psalm 8, 135
    from Psalm 42, 135
    from Psalm 90, 136
    Psalm 121, 137
Putnam, Samuel (translator), 109

QUARLES, FRANCIS
    "A Good-Night," 166

RALEGH, WALTER
    from "The Passionate Mans Pilgrimage," 185–86
Rauschenberg, Robert, 6, 7
"Remember" (Rossetti), 109
"Requiem" (Rilke), 80
"Requiem" (Stevenson), 110
"Returning to Friedrichskoog" (Prufer), 181–82
Rexroth, Kenneth (translator), 48, 49
RICH, ADRIENNE
    "Final Notations," 209–10
    "Tattered Kaddish," 64–65
Richard II (Shakespeare), 105
RILKE, RAINER MARIA
    "Buddha in Glory," 157
    I love the dark hours of my being, 208–9
    from "Requiem," 80
ROBINSON, MARILYNNE
    from *The Death of Adam*, 87
ROETHKE, THEODORE
    "In a Dark Time," 66–67
    from "The Lost Son," 87–88
ROSSETTI, CHRISTINA
    "Remember," 109

Rossetti, Dante Gabriel (translator), 102
Rubáiyát of Omar Khayyám, The (Fitzgerald, translator), 165
RUKEYSER, MURIEL
    from "The Sun-Artist," 180–81

"Sailing to Byzantium" (Yeats), 155
Sappho
    But I claim, 90
    "Epitaph," 94
"Self-Reliance" (Emerson), 112
SEXTON, ANNE
    "The Fury of Guitars and Sopranos," 202–3
SHAKESPEARE, WILLIAM
    "Dirge," from *Cymbeline*, 167–68
    from *Hamlet*, 106
    Jonson on, 106–7
    from *Julius Caesar*, 76, 105
    from *Richard II*, 105
    Song, from *Henry VIII*, 167
    from *The Tempest*, 168
SHELLEY, PERCY BYSSHE
    from "Adonais: An Elegy on the Death of John Keats," 45–
        46, 152–54
    "To____," 164
Sherrard, Philip, 15, 97
"Ship of Death" (Lawrence), 190–91
sister, readings for remembering, 214
SMITH, STEVIE
    "By a Holm-Oak," 60–61
SNYDER, GARY
    Stay together, 184
"So, We'll Go No More A-Roving" (Byron), 20–21
Solace of Open Spaces, The (Ehrlich), 176–77
"Soliloquy on Immortality" (Cato), 72
"Song for the Last Act" (Bogan), 206–7
SOPHOCLES
    from *Oedipus the King*, 100
SPENSER, EDMUND
    from *The Faerie Queen*, 162
spiritual, 61

"Spring and Fall: To a Young Child" (Hopkins), 18
Staniforth, Maxwell (translator), 76
Stay together (Snyder), 184
STEVENS, WALLACE
    "Of Mere Being," 210–11
    from "Peter Quince at the Clavier," 181
STEVENSON, ROBERT LOUIS
    "Requiem," 110
STRAND, MARK
    "The End," 198–99
"Sun-Artist, The" (Rukeyser), 180–81
Susini, E., 77
"Swift's Epitaph" (Yeats), 115
SWINBURNE, ALGERNON CHARLES
    from "The Garden of Proserpine," 172

Tao Te Ching (Lao-Tzu), 143
"Tattered Kaddish" (Rich), 64–65
Tell him that we shall all bear his memory (Hunt), 77–78
Tempest, The (Shakespeare), 168
TENNYSON, ALFRED, LORD
    from "Crossing the Bar," 166
    from *Idylls of the King*, 102–4
    I have suffered more than ever I thought I could, 43
"The bustle in a house" (Dickinson), 19–20
"The friends of my father" (Menashe), 123–24
The Lord giveth, the Lord taketh away (*The Union Prayerbook*),
    132–33
The mists rise over (Akahito), 49
The moon and the year (Maya poem), 81
The only possible proof of the existence of water (Bachelard, quot-
    ing Susini), 77
There be many shapes of mystery (Euripides), 14
There is nothing more terrible (Kurata, translator), 46–47
"There's a certain slant of light" (Dickinson), 19
The servants, the pomp, have vanished (Emperor Hanazono), 48
This Wild Darkness (Brodkey), 192–95
THOMAS, DYLAN, 2
    "Do not go gentle into that good night," 65–66
"Those Winter Sundays" (Hayden), 124

Thou hast come safe to port (lyric written for the Abbess of
        Grandestine), 161
"Threnody" (Emerson), 44–45
THUCYDIDES
        from *History of the Peloponnesian War*, 97–100
"Time does not bring relief" (Millay), 62
"To___" (Shelley), 164
TOLSTOY, LEO
        from *What Men Live By*, 20
"To the memory of my beloved, the author, Master William Shake-
        speare, and what he hath left us" (Jonson), 106–7
"Tract" (Williams), 29–31
Twain, Mark, 1

"Union of Friends" (Penn), 140
Union Prayerbook, The
        from funeral services, 15–16, 132–33
        from the Yom Kippur morning service, 35
Upanishads, The, 144–46

"Vacillation" (Yeats), 160
VAN DOREN, MARK
        "What Now?," 32
VAUGHAN, HENRY
        from "Friends Departed," 151
        from "The Night," 152
VERVAET, KAREN
        from "Karen's Journal, 3 April 1993," 191–92
VILLON, FRANÇOIS
        "The Ballad of Dead Ladies," 101–2
VIRGIL
        from *The Aeneid*, 100
"Virtue" (Herbert), 148
"Voice, The" (Hardy), 56–57

"Walk, The" (Hardy), 56
WATSON, CLYDE
        "Portrait (modelled after ee cummings)," 125

WATSON, NANCY DINGMAN
    "You came to me," 125–26
WATTS, ISAAC
    from "O God, Our Help," 142
Way of Man, The (Buber), 78–79
Weil, Simone, 3
"We'll to the Woods No More" (Housman), 21
WELTY, EUDORA
    from *One Writer's Beginnings*, 175
    from *The Optimist's Daughter*, 207–8
"We Spirits Dance" (Wintu), 51
We were together (Yakamochi), 49
What Men Live By (Tolstoy), 20
"What Now?" (Van Doren), 32
"When lilacs last in the dooryard bloom'd" (Whitman),
    171–72
WHITMAN, WALT
    from "A Clear Midnight," 23
    "A March in the Ranks Hard-Prest, and the Road Un-
        known," 112–14
    Be not curious about God, 78
    "The Last Invocation," 189
    from "When lilacs last in the dooryard bloom'd," 171–72
WHITTIER, JOHN GREENLEAF
    from "The Eternal Goodness," 141
"Widower, The" (Kipling), 115–16
"Widow's Lament in Springtime, The" (Williams), 116–17
wife, readings for remembering, 214
WILDE, LADY
    "The Black Lamb," 85
WILLIAMS, WILLIAM CARLOS
    "El Hombre," 209
    "The Widow's Lament in Springtime," 116–17
    "Tract," 29–31
WILSON, JOHN (CHRISTOPHER NORTH)
    from "A Fairy's Funeral," 27–28
WINTU
    "We Spirits Dance," 51
Wittgenstein, Ludwig, 3
WOLFE, CHARLES
    from "The Burial of Sir John Moore at Coruña," 109–10

WOLLSTONECRAFT, MARY
        Dream that my little baby came to life again, 43
"Words for a Totem Animal" (Merwin), 197–98
WORDSWORTH, DOROTHY
        from *Journal*, 22–23
WORDSWORTH, WILLIAM
        from "Lines Composed a Few Miles Above Tintern Abbey,"
                169–70
        from "Ode: Intimations of Immortality from Recollections of
                Early Childhood," 154–55

YAKAMOCHI
        We were together, 49
YAMATOHIME, EMPRESS
        Others may forget you, 49
YEATS, W. B., 85
        from "Fergus and the Druid," 174–75
        from "Sailing to Byzantium," 155
        from "Swift's Epitaph," 115
        from "Vacillation," 160
Yom Kippur morning service (*The Union Prayerbook*), 35
"You came to me" (Watson), 125–26
You were always changing into something else (O'Hara), 196

Credits